"I do ... *appointment with you?"*

He barked the words curtly, rapidly recovering from having appeared momentarily rocked.

Appointment! Yancie fumed; she was angry, not to mention a bundle of nerves into the bargain. Perhaps that was why, when she had half decided not to mention his proposal if he didn't remember it, that she'd snapped back bluntly, "That's no way to speak to your fiancée!"

Thomson stared back at her, his expression positively staggered.

Yancie didn't know which of them was the more shocked. What she did know, though, was that this was the first he'd heard of it—or wanted to hear of it.

THE MARRIAGE PLEDGE

For three cousins it has to be marriage—
pure and simple!

Yancie, Fennia and Astra are cousins—
exceedingly close cousins, who've grown up together
and shared the same experiences. For all of them,
one thing is certain: they'll never be like their mothers,
having serial, meaningless affairs. They've pledged that,
for them, it has to be marriage—or nothing!

Meet Yancie
this month in
THE FEISTY FIANCÉE

The Feisty Fiancée

Jessica Steele

THE MARRIAGE PLEDGE

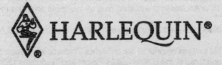
HARLEQUIN®

TORONTO • NEW YORK • LONDON
AMSTERDAM • PARIS • SYDNEY • HAMBURG
STOCKHOLM • ATHENS • TOKYO • MILAN • MADRID
PRAGUE • WARSAW • BUDAPEST • AUCKLAND

ISBN 0-373-03588-8

THE FEISTY FIANCÉE

First North American Publication 2000.

CHAPTER ONE

IT WAS the first job she'd ever had, and she loved it. Yancie steered the Mercedes onto the motorway and in next to no time was in the fast lane speeding to pick up her passenger.

Not that there should have been any need to pile on the speed. Had she in fact been where she was supposed to be she would not have needed to be driving anywhere at all.

That was the only snag with this job—there was a lot of waiting around. She wasn't used to waiting around; she was used to be being busy. Truth to tell though, the hanging around hadn't proved any great problem. Not after the first week anyhow. She had only been in the job for three weeks, but after the first week of dropping off some high-up executive or other in the Addison Kirk Group and being told she would be required again in two hours, or three hours' time, whenever, Yancie had come to the conclusion she had better things to do than hang around cooling her heels.

Everything had worked out perfectly after that.

She visited museums, art galleries and cinemas, stopped by to call on friends if she happened to be anywhere within a twenty-mile radius. And even on one occasion she had been able to call in on her mother—taking care of course to first remove the identifying label complete with photograph—Yancie Dawkins—she was supposed to wear at all times on the jacket of her uniform. Bubbles to that!

Yancie was very much aware that her mother would not like it at all if she ever found out she had not only left her home, where she'd lived with her stepfather, but had actually found herself a job. She had once vaguely mooted that she wouldn't mind a career in something; her mother had been scandalised.

It made for an easier life if she said nothing, Yancie mused, and smiled as she thought few people she knew would be brave enough to risk her mother's wrath by enlightening her.

Yancie took a quick glance to the seat beside her where the identifying tag lay. She must remember to put it on again before she picked up today's executive, Mr Clements.

She motored on at speed, reflecting on how the job had more found her than she had found it. Though in actual fact it was her cousin, Greville, to be more accurate, who had found it for her. And, if she was going to be even more precise, Greville, her half-cousin.

Though she loved him to bits, as her 'full' cousins also did. But Yancie was a good driver and was able to be totally aware of her surroundings, to anticipate any sudden moves other drivers might make, while at the same time reflecting on past events.

It had not been to her own mother she had gone when, pride ruling, she had left the comfortable home she shared with her stepfather and his daughter four weeks ago, but to Aunt Delia, Greville's mother.

Of course, Yancie admitted, she should never have let Suzannah Lloyd borrow her car. She wouldn't have had she known Sukey was going to turn it over and cause it to be a write-off. Having assured herself that Sukey was all right and that nobody else was hurt, Yancie had told her stepfather what had happened.

Ralph Proctor was a super stepfather, but, anticipating his concern, like hers, would initially be all for Sukey, to Yancie's surprise, he'd instead grown quite cross and begun to give her a lecture about lending her car to all and sundry.

Yancie might well have taken this telling-off as her due. But, unfortunately, Ralph's daughter, Estelle, had been there and she'd staggered Yancie completely by challenging that she hoped Yancie wouldn't expect her father to pay for a new car for her.

Yancie wasn't the only one who was surprised—her stepfather had looked startled too at the nastiness in his daughter's tone. Though before he could find his voice Yancie was proudly asserting. 'I wouldn't dream of it! I've enough money from my allowance to...'

'The allowance you take from my father!' Estelle reminded her waspishly—and Yancie was left staring at her.

'I never asked for an allowance!' was the best defence Yancie could find.

'You don't mind taking it, though, do you?' Estelle attacked—and that was when Yancie suddenly and abruptly realised that her stepfather's house was not big enough for both her and her stepsister. She'd had no idea that Estelle resented her so much!

'Not any more,' Yancie said quietly, and was on her way, in no mind to stay and listen to her stepfather transferring his crossness onto his daughter.

'Really, Estelle!' she heard him say as she left the drawing room and turned to close the door behind her. 'You know full well that Yancie more than earns her allowance with the work she does keeping this place running smoothly.'

'Advertise for a housekeep—'

Yancie didn't wait to hear any more. She couldn't stay after this, she just couldn't! She went, where she and her cousins Fennia and Astra went in bad times and good; she went to see her aunt, Delia.

'I never did like Estelle Proctor,' Delia Alford opined when Yancie relayed all that had taken place.

'It is true, though.' Yancie tried to be fair. 'I have never minded taking an allowance from Ralph.'

'You've worked for it!' Delia exclaimed, knowing positively how, four years ago, when, at aged eighteen, Yancie and her two cousins had left boarding-school, while the other two had gone into higher business training, Ralph Proctor had almost begged Yancie to stay home and take over the running of his over-large house—her mother had sanctioned it, because it was what she termed 'not a proper job'. 'With that daughter of his picking fault all the time, you know as well as I that he couldn't keep a housekeeper for five minutes. And Estelle won't want to take over—the only comfort that jealous madam's interested in, is her own.'

'What shall I do?'

'What do you want to do?'

Yancie thought about it. She loved her stepfather dearly, but... 'I don't want to go back,' she realised. 'Estelle has never been the easiest person to live with; after that...'

'You don't have to go back,' Delia Alford assured her firmly, going on, everything cut and dried to her way of thinking, 'You're more than welcome to live here with me, you know that. Though Astra will want you to move in with her. She has more than enough room at her flat, and you know Fennia would be delighted for you to move in with them too.'

The flat her two cousins lived in belonged to Astra's

father in actual fact, but he preferred to live in Barbados rather than the elegant apartment which was in a smart part of London. Astra had welcomed Fennia living with her, since Christmas—only a few weeks ago—when Fennia's mother had caught the older woman's latest boyfriend with his arms around Fennia and had chosen to see it as her daughter leading him on. She had, not too politely, thrown Fennia out.

Yancie was in the middle of saying that she'd give Astra a ring, and also that since she just couldn't possibly touch another penny of her stepfather's money she would get a job, when her cousin Greville arrived on one of his unscheduled visits to see his mother.

'Little Yancie Dawkins!' he smiled, having greeted his mother, opening his arms wide for Yancie the way he had since the days when she was a toddler.

Yancie went over to her half-cousin, who was nearing forty and a most reliable figure in her somewhat trauma-ridden life. Greville gave her a hug and a kiss, and then asked what was this diabolical talk he'd overheard about her getting a job.

Over a cup of coffee Yancie and his mother filled him in on the happenings of that morning. 'I should have done something about a job before this,' Yancie realised.

'You know your mother's not going to like it, don't you?' Greville commented. 'She'll give both you and Ralph hell!'

'Oh, heck, I never thought about my mother,' Yancie answered, feeling suddenly wretched. It was significant, she supposed, that Aunt Delia had not suggested she might make her home with her mother. The novelty of having a little girl, a white-haired child, had soon worn off. Yancie and her two cousins, who had been similar hindrances to the respective mothers, were, at the age of seven, sent off to boarding-school.

Yancie drove automatically as she recalled how her father had died in a skiing accident and how, although he had left her mother well provided for, it hadn't taken her mother long to run through his fortune. To find herself a job had simply never entered Ursula Dawkins' head. She had instead, after having affairs with several possibles, elected to marry money in the person of Ralph Proctor.

Yancie, on her holiday visits home, had learned to greatly care for Ralph Proctor, and he in turn had grown very fond of her. Too fond, anyhow, to consider allowing Yancie to live anywhere but in his home after the inevitable happened and his marriage broke down. Which was quite all right by Ursula Proctor, who walked off with a very handsome divorce settlement without the encumbrance of a too beautiful ash-blonde daughter to cramp her style.

That wouldn't stop her mother, Yancie fretted, from attempting to make her life, and Ralph's life, a misery should she learn that not only was her daughter no longer under Ralph Proctor's roof, but was actually working.

Although on that fateful day she had left her stepfather's home, Yancie had had no idea what work she could do. 'The thing is, I'm not properly trained for anything in particular,' she explained to her aunt and half-cousin. 'I can housekeep, I suppose, but...'

'You can't do that!' Delia Alford stated categorically.

'It's all I know,' Yancie confessed.

'Nonsense!' her aunt declared stoutly. 'You can drive, and you can...'

'There's a driving job vacant at Addison Kirk,'

Greville chipped in, and halted when both his mother and cousin looked at him. 'But you wouldn't want to do that...'

'Oh, yes, I would!' Yancie jumped at the chance.

'Hey! I wasn't serious!' Greville protested.

'I am,' Yancie answered.

'I'm not sure they want a woman driver...' he began to prevaricate. Though when his two female relatives looked at him askance he had the grace to grin as he conceded, 'But, perhaps, in these times of equal opportunities, it's time they had one.'

Greville then went on to outline how one of the senior drivers had retired at the end of December and how his replacement hadn't stayed in the job longer than a week, and Aunt Delia beamed. She was very proud of her son; he, as his father had been before him, was on the board of Addison Kirk.

'That's settled, then,' she stated, and, smiling at her son, she added, 'What's the point of you being on the board if you can't give your little cousin a helping hand?'

His 'little cousin' was five feet eight, but as she looked uncertainly at him so he too smiled. 'Indeed,' he agreed, 'what point?'

And so, after the formality of an interview—the outcome of which she knew in advance—Yancie had got the job. As to the politics of the matter, Greville had instructed the head of personnel to make no written mention of his interest, and Greville—while certain his cousin would fare well with her fellow workers—had suggested to her that it might be an idea not to mention that she had obtained the job through him.

'In fact,' he'd smiled, 'it might be an idea if you didn't mention the family connection at all.'

So she hadn't, and inside a few weeks she had gone from not having a car to drive to having a Mercedes, a Jaguar and any number of other cars in which to visit her friends.

As far as Yancie's mother was concerned, having learned that Sukey Lloyd had written off Yancie's car, to Yancie's astonishment, had naturally assumed that the Jaguar Yancie had driven the day she'd called was a replacement.

Yancie's immediate superior had given her a very intensive driving test before stating that her driving was up to his high standard. She had then been measured for a hurriedly tailored uniform—two jackets, two skirts in brown and several shirts in beige, bearing the brown embroidered Addison Kirk logo of a bridge spanning the world. Yancie supposed the logo to be something to do with the manufacture of industrial material which the company seemed mainly concerned with. But so long as she could hide the logo underneath a brooch of some sort when she was visiting friends she didn't much mind what the firm did. She didn't want to risk anyone she knew bumping into her mother and giving a hint that her daughter was now earning a wage.

Yancie executed a neat piece of lane-swapping and went back to reflecting how, as her aunt had said, her cousins had wanted her to move in with them.

'Don't you dare think of living anywhere but with us,' red-haired Astra had declared warmly.

'I second the motion,' grinned black-haired Fennia— and it was just like being at boarding-school again, only better. The three cousins had been born within a month of each other and were as close as sisters. Closer, in fact, than were the three sisters who had borne them.

But, love her mother, her aunt Portia and her aunt

Imogen though she did, Yancie didn't want to think of
them in any depth. Between them these three ladies had
managed to give them enough hang-ups to dwell on.

Thankfully, just at that moment Yancie spotted that
the petrol gauge on the dashboard was pointing to
empty. Oh, crumbs—she'd never make it back to
London. It was doubtful she'd have enough juice to
make it back to pick up Mr Clements!

Yancie at that moment immediately recognised that
she was about to drive past a service station. Lord knew
when she might come across another one! There was no
time to think, only to act. Quickly she spun the wheel
and was already crossing into the next lane when a vi-
olently blasted car horn alerted her to the fact that she
had very nearly rammed an Aston Martin.

Oh, grief. She'd noticed it earlier but, since the
driver—with all that power under the bonnet—hadn't
wanted to overtake, she'd stayed in the fast lane and had
paid little more attention. But now she'd not time to
apologize, only time to get out of trouble, and swiftly!

Fortunately, the driver of the Aston Martin reacted
quickly and moved out of harm's way—and Yancie
made it safely to the forecourt of the self-service petrol
station.

She would have liked to blame her inattentive driving
not only on the sudden realisation that she was driving
on empty, but also on the fact that thinking of her mother
and her two aunts was invariably upsetting. But she
knew she had only herself to blame—she and she alone
was at fault.

Yancie stepped out of the Mercedes, but had barely
got the driver's door closed when the Aston Martin
pulled in behind her and, breathing fire from every
pore—if his expression was anything to go by—a tall,

dark-haired man began heading her way. By the look of it, she was going to have to apologise!

And she might have done but—hold on a minute—her livelihood—not to mention this lovely job—was at stake here. She had no idea how these things worked, but if this immaculately suited man bearing down on her made a note of her registration number and reported her she could, ultimately, lose her job! In the wrong though she was, she just couldn't afford to admit it—to apologise.

'What the *hell* do you think you're playing at?' the man challenged aggressively the moment he was next to her, hard, unimpressed grey eyes flicking over her slender shape, taking in the brooch she wore—thank goodness she had covered up the firm's logo—you never knew who might recognise it!

But she wasn't used to being spoken to like that. 'Me!' she retaliated. 'Why, you grumpy old devil,' she charged of the mid-thirties-looking man who still breathed fire and brimstone. 'If you weren't so keen to be the centre of attention in your Aston Martin, you'd have been in the correct motorway lane, and not riding on my bumper...'

Oh, my word, he didn't like being called a grumpy old devil, did he—or any of the rest of it! 'I *was* in the correct lane!' he snarled, his jaw jutting. 'Not only did you not give the smallest indication of your intention to cross straight in front of me...'

'I haven't time to stand here all day bandying words with you!' she cut in arrogantly—and saw his eyes narrow at her tone. Quite clearly, Mr-High-and-Mighty-Aston-Martin wasn't used to being spoken to in such a way. She saw him take a sharp intake of controlling breath.

Then, his jaw jutting no less furiously, he gritted, 'I'll attend to you later,' and turned sharply away and went striding back to the rather superb-looking Aston Martin.

There was nothing he could possibly do, Yancie told herself ten minutes later. His 'I'll attend to you later' had no teeth. What could he do for goodness' sake? It was a cold day, but, thanks to an efficient car heater, she had shed her uniform jacket. She'd removed that identifying tag when she'd left Mr Clements, and had pinned a rather attractive brooch over the Addison Kirk logo on her shirt, so sucks boo! The only way he might be able to trace her was if he'd thought to note her car registration number—but, even then, that near-ghastly accident was purely his word against hers—so he could take his 'I'll attend to you later' and sling it. So why was she still trembling?

Yancie proceeded on her way with the utmost care after that. The incident had shaken her more than she would have liked to admit. She was, however, correctly uniformed, with her identifying appendage neatly in place, when, with five minutes to spare, she arrived to wait for Mr Clements.

Very occasionally, when she was working quite late, Yancie had permission—after first dropping off her passenger at his address—to take whichever motor she was driving on to her own home. She'd had to assure her immediate boss, Kevin Veasey, that she was able to garage the car, but even then this concession was only allowed on the understanding she would not avail herself of it for her personal use.

She was late that night, so took the Mercedes home. As late as it was, her cousin Astra was still out working. 'Astra works too hard,' she remarked to her other lovely cousin, Fennia.

'She loves it,' Fennia answered. 'Had a good day?'

'Given I nearly wrote off an Aston Martin with a Mercedes, can't complain,' she smiled, and shared the experience with her cousin over a sumptuous casserole Fennia had made while waiting for her two cousins to come home.

'Men!' Fennia opined.

'I was in the wrong,' Yancie pointed out.

'I know! But—*men*!'

They laughed. They'd roomed together, the three cousins, at boarding-school. They'd shared each other's secrets, mopped up—in the early days—each other's tears when their mothers had hopped from relationship to relationship. Stable backgrounds—forget it! They'd had so many 'uncles', it had needed a young mind to keep up with it.

They'd tried hard not to be judgmental, but it had been just a touch embarrassing not knowing which 'uncle' had been coming with their mothers to pick them up at each term-end.

Aunt Delia was the rock they'd each leaned towards. Aunt Delia had been ten years old when her widowed mother had remarried, and in three years had produced three daughters. It was the younger girls' dreadfully strict upbringing, Aunt Delia had explained, by a father who seemed to have few sensitivities, that was responsible for the way each of her half-sisters, in turn, had rebelled. Yancie's mother apparently had been well 'off the rails' before Yancie's father had been killed. Fennia's mother was twice married—and on the look-out for husband number three. And Astra's mother had twice divorced and was at present living with someone.

With that kind of a background, the three cousins had been sixteen when, fearing they might have inherited

some wayward gene from their mothers, they had vowed
that they were going to guard with everything they had
against turning out like their mothers. They wanted nothing of their mothers' explosive and sometimes quite awful relationships which—in the main—brought nothing
but disaster.

To date, six years on, it hadn't been a problem. In
general the cousins had nothing against men. And so far,
thank goodness, none of them had felt the smallest inclination to be wayward where men were concerned.
Though it was true that if they ever went out on a date
and did dip their toes in unchartered, experimental wa-
ters it was mainly with someone fairly safe whom they'd
known for ages—usually the brother or relation of someone with whom they'd been at boarding-school.

Yancie drove to work the following morning growing
more and more comfortable with her lot. She was still
in frequent telephone contact with her stepfather—who
now employed a housekeeper—but she still had no wish
to return to live in the same house as Estelle. Yancie
enjoyed living again with her cousins. Fennia, despite
her business training, thoroughly enjoyed the job she had
found working with toddlers in a day nursery, and Astra,
the most academic of the three of them, was working all
hours as a financial adviser, and loving it.

Yancie drove into the vast garages of the Addison
Kirk Group and exchanged her uniform jacket and neat
shoes for a pair of Wellingtons and an over-large over-
all.

The men she worked with were getting more and more
used to seeing her about the place. But even though—
as she unreeled the water hose prior to tackling the wheel
arches on yesterday's Mercedes—she knew she must
look a sketch in her present outfit it still didn't prevent

one courageous colleague from commenting, 'You still look terrific even in that get-up!'

She had no wish to be thought stand-offish. 'You reckon?' she answered.

'There's no substitute for style—and you've got it, plus,' he stated, and looked so serious, she had to laugh—which caused him to ask her for a date.

Her laugh faded. 'I never mix business with pleasure,' she replied, and turned away to concentrate on turning the water on.

She was happily absorbed in her task when Wilf Fisher, one of the mechanics and a family man, came over to thank her for going out of her way to drop a spare electric kettle off to his mother yesterday.

'It was a pleasure,' she assured him, though it had been a fifty-mile round trip on which she headed as soon as she'd seen Mr Clements safely to his destination.

'I couldn't have got it to her before tomorrow otherwise,' he explained again. 'And, well, quite honestly, the wife does get a little bit fed up with me having to drive up there to sort the old dear out all the time.'

Yancie sympathised; she knew all about mothers and their urgent summonses. 'Think nothing of it,' she smiled. 'Any time.'

Wilf went on his way, clearly feeling better for her offer of 'Any time', and Yancie, her smile fading, fell to thinking how, if she hadn't been where she shouldn't yesterday, then she wouldn't have had that run-in—very nearly literally—with Mr Aston Martin.

She owned that the near calamity had truly unnerved her. For all she had made light of it to Fennia, and to Astra too when she had come home, Yancie had not been able to get to sleep last night for thinking about it. She had so nearly caused a very serious accident. And, to make matters worse, when the driver of the other car had followed her to remonstrate with her, what had she done but called him a grumpy old devil and accused him, totally falsely, of being in the wrong lane?

She had been in the wrong, Yancie knew that. Apart from the fact the 'grumpy old devil' wasn't old at all— why couldn't she get the memory of his face out of her head? She knew she'd know him again anywhere—not that she would see him again. She must have been in a panic yesterday when she had thought that he'd find out more about her from the car registration number. Records of that nature were difficult to access, weren't they? And, in any case, everything about him had spoken of him being some kind of executive. This morning she doubted he'd have time to bother contacting the police about an accident that had never happened.

Yancie usually had quite a few driving jobs on a Friday. But this Friday, although she caught Kevin Veasey looking over to her several times, he didn't have even one task for her.

She kept busy, however, washing cars, going for sandwiches or running any other errand anyone wanted doing. Then at three o'clock, to her delight, she got the plummiest job of them all. Word had come down, from the head of the whole outfit, no less, that her presence was requested on the top floor at four o'clock.

She had never driven Thomson Wakefield before. Indeed, she had never so much as clapped eyes on him. In fact, having worked for Addison's for three weeks now, she had been beginning to suspect—to the blazes with any sex discrimination law—that old Mr Wakefield would die rather than let some female drive him.

But, not so! Why she thought Thomson Wakefield must be old, she couldn't have said. Probably because it didn't seem likely that someone still wet behind the ears would have the honour of holding his exalted position.

But what was she bothering her head with such thoughts for? He wanted her to drive him—*her*! Inwardly beaming, Yancie, after her car-washing activities, would have loved to have taken a shower before she presented herself on the top floor.

Not to worry, though; she had a fresh shirt in her locker, and a quick freshen-up of her make-up and a comb run through her shoulder-length ash-blonde hair, and she'd be as good as new.

It puzzled her when, at half past three, hair combed, fresh lipstick applied, she went and asked Kevin what car she would be driving and he replied he'd had no instructions yet about where she was going. His instructions were that she present herself at four.

'I'll sort a vehicle out when I come back,' she decided. Given the choice, she fancied the Jaguar, but, of course, Mr Wakefield might have his own preference.

Yancie made her way to the top floor with her head filled with speculations on how far afield the chief man might want to be driven. Working overtime never bothered her, so if he had it in mind to be driven up to Scotland that was all right by her—though she'd have to ring either Astra or Fennia to tell them not to expect her home.

All of which was just so much flight of fancy, she smiled to herself as, finding the door she was looking for, she knocked lightly and went in.

'Yancie Dawkins?' enquired the woman in her mid-forties Kevin had told her was Thomas Wakefield's PA.

'That's right,' Yancie answered easily, her upbringing and education making her feel perfectly at ease in any company. 'Mr Wakefield is expecting me.'

'If you'd like to take a seat,' Veronica Taylor suggested pleasantly.

Yancie took the seat indicated, and waited. And waited. Four-fifteen came and went—and still she waited. 'Does Mr Wakefield know I'm here?' she asked his PA.

'Oh, yes,' his PA answered, her tone as pleasant as ever.

Four-thirty came—and went. Wishing she'd brought a book to read, Yancie wondered if perhaps the great man had been held up on a phone call. For thirty minutes!

Another ten minutes passed, by which time Yancie had gone from feeling completely at ease to feeling just a shade uncomfortable. Okay, so he was a busy man, but… *Be patient, he's paying you, and you need this job.* Hang it all, she loved her job. It wasn't taxing on the brain—but who needed taxing? The freedom the job allowed was limitless. Indeed, it didn't seem like a job of work at all.

Even so, having cautioned herself to be patient, when another few minutes of her having absolutely nothing to do went by, Yancie was considering telling Veronica Taylor to ring down to the garage and let her know when the old man surfaced. Then Yancie heard sounds on the other side of the door she'd assumed connected the two offices—and that reassured her that the old boy hadn't expired while she waited.

She pinned a 'Yes, sir' look on her face—it cost nothing—and the door opened. So too did her mouth. More—her jaw dropped. Oh, no! It couldn't be! She didn't believe it! She just *didn't* believe it.

Horrified, Yancie saw at once that 'old' Mr Thomson Wakefield, for this surely must be he, was not old at all!

He was tall, dark-haired, had hard grey eyes—and was somewhere in his mid-thirties. She had thought she had never clapped eyes on him before—but she had! Even minus his Aston Martin—she recognised him.

Oh, mother! Yancie stared, wanting to die, at the grim, unsmiling countenance of the man standing there coldly surveying her—a man who clearly had no intention of making things easy for her. She tried hard to sort her brain patterns out, to think up some kind of defence. But what defence was there?

So much for her hiding the firm's logo on her shirt yesterday—a fact he hadn't missed, she was suddenly positive. This man—this man, who'd made it to the top of his tree—was, she all at once knew, a man from which little escaped. What he didn't know, she just knew, he troubled to find out.

This man knew, as he'd known yesterday, exactly what her brooch had concealed. Though he hadn't needed to see the Addison Kirk logo; he'd probably recognised the car she had been driving. In all probability he had only very recently—perhaps even the day before—been a passenger in it!

'Mr Wakefield?' she enquired, hoping there was some wonderful mistake and that this man—this man who yesterday, by his swift and skilful reactions, had managed to avoid what would have been an almighty collision—and earned a load of lip from her for his trouble—was not, by some miracle, the head of the Addison Kirk Group.

He didn't bother to confirm but, ignoring her completely, instructed his PA, 'Hold my calls for five minutes, please.' She had called him a grumpy old devil—it was going to take that long?

He held his office door open for her to go through.

Yancie stood up, uncertain whether or not to walk to the other door, and keep on walking. 'I'll attend to you later', this man had yesterday threatened—he must have pegged her as employed by the company before he'd even said it. 'Later', Yancie knew, had just arrived—but she wasn't the sort to run away.

CHAPTER TWO

YANCIE crossed into Thomson Wakefield's office. It was large and, as well as having the usual office furnishings, also housed a comfortable-looking sofa, and a couple of easy chairs grouped around a low coffee table.

She had thought his dismissal of her from the company he headed would take seconds; she would have preferred it. But, no. Not the most talkative of men she had ever known, he pointed to a chair on the other side of his large desk.

She took the seat and while he sat facing her so she began to gather her scattered wits. Without question she was to be well and truly carpeted—she guessed few had called the head man a grumpy old devil—apart from all the rest that had gone with it—and got away with it. It surprised her that he hadn't just instructed Kevin Veasey to sack her and be done with it.

That he hadn't instructed Kevin gave her a ray of hope. She hung onto it. She loved her job. 'I suppose you aren't very interested in an apology,' she opened politely when Thomson Wakefield, saying not one word, continued to study her as if she were some strange object on the end of a pin.

'Are you sorry?' he asked crisply.

Yesterday—forget it. Today—abjectly. To keep this job, she could be grovellingly sorry. Well, perhaps that was going a bit far—but she was prepared to go as far as pride would allow.

'I don't normally behave like that,' she said prettily.

'You mean you don't normally very nearly cause a disaster, then refuse to accept blame?'

Yancie knew there and then that this man gave no quarter. A hint of a smile would do wonders for that unsmiling, sombre, see-nothing-to-laugh-at, though in actual fact quite good-looking face.

'I was in the wrong—on both counts.' She did a swift about-turn from her attitude of yesterday.

'Your driving was appalling!' Thomson Wakefield agreed stonily.

'Not all the time!' she dared to argue, saw that hadn't gone down well, and added swiftly, 'Up until that point, when I suddenly realised I was driving on an empty fuel tank, my driving was first-class.' She'd be modest tomorrow—today her job was on the line—not to say by a gossamer thread.

He nodded as if conceding her point. 'I'd been tracking you for some miles,' he openly let her know.

That jolted her. Oh, why hadn't somebody told her that the boss man had an Aston Martin? It might have clicked when she'd first become aware of the car yesterday, might have given her a chance to think she should take some kind of action. Well, possibly not. 'You pegged me as one of yours miles before our—er—introduction?' she enquired.

Thomson Wakefield studied her for some seconds without speaking, his glance taking in her almost white ash-blonde hair, her bluest of blue eyes, her dainty features and perfect skin.

'You're different from the rest of our drivers, I'll give you that,' he pronounced curtly, leaving her to guess whether he meant that she had started to ask questions in what was his interview, or if he meant her feminine features.

She opted for the latter. 'I'm the only female driver this particular part of the group has,' she commented. 'Ah!' she exclaimed as light dawned. 'But you already knew that.'

'It took but a few moments for my PA to discover which female driver in our livery was on that stretch of the motorway yesterday,' he conceded coolly.

Uh-oh. If he knew that much, it was pretty certain he also knew that she shouldn't have been anywhere near that section of the motorway yesterday! Yancie sensed even more trouble. Although, fingers crossed, he still hadn't said those diabolical words she didn't want to hear—You're out. Though it could be, of course, that, after giving her a tongue-lashing—let him try—he had plans for Kevin Veasey to tell her she had washed her last car at Addison Kirk. Somebody had almost certainly instructed Kevin not to let her take any of the vehicles out that day; of that Yancie all at once realised she could be certain. Silence, just then, however, seemed the better part of discretion.

'So,' Thomson Wakefield went on, 'perhaps, Miss Dawkins, you would care to tell me your version of the events yesterday. The events that led up to you almost demolishing not one motor vehicle, but two—leaving aside the perilous way you very nearly dispatched the two of us into the next world.'

Well, no, actually, I wouldn't. But he was waiting. 'It's very kind of you to give me a fair hearing—er—in the circumstances,' she smiled; he had no charm, so she tried him with some of hers.

Water off a duck's back! Those grey eyes were staying on her, and were noting her smile, her lovely even teeth—her boarding-school had been most particular about teeth—but Yancie soon saw that not by so much as a flicker of an eyelash was he to be charmed.

'So?' He was waiting.

'Well, as I mentioned, I suddenly saw that I was driving with a nearly empty tank.' Silence, he was still waiting; it forced her to go on. 'It was then that, simultaneously, I realised several things.' Silence. Oh, bubbles to it! If she'd known for certain that she was going to be out of a job after all this, Yancie was sure she would have packed it in right then. But hope sprang eternal—so she ploughed on. 'At the same time as realising I was driving on a nearly empty tank, I realised I wouldn't have enough juice to get me back to London, let alone to pick up Mr C—' Yancie broke off abruptly. Oh, grief, she shouldn't have been driving *to* pick up Mr Clements, she should have been *there*, waiting. 'S-so…' Damn that stutter, this man was making her nervous—it had never happened before—and she didn't like it. 'And—er—and then, coincidentally, I saw the "services" sign and there just wasn't time to think…'

'Merely to act!' Thomson Wakefield butted in sharply.

Who was telling this, her or him? With a start of surprise, Yancie realised that she was beginning to get angry. She seldom, if ever, got angry. Though, having been left cooling her heels for near enough forty-five minutes while waiting for this man to deign to see her, perhaps, she considered, getting a little angry was justified.

Though hang on a minute. Didn't she truly want this job? Yes, she did. 'You're right, of course.' She tried another charm-filled smile—that had absolutely, one hundred per cent not the slightest effect on the stern-faced individual opposite. 'I was wrong, wrong, totally wrong to cross over into your lane the way I did,' she added hurriedly. 'It was a momentary lapse of attention.

And I promise you I have never, ever, driven so care-
lessly before. Nor will I ever again,' she further promised, having in fact learned a very salutary lesson yesterday, but hoping he didn't think she was laying it on
with a trowel.

Thomson Wakefield had nothing to say for many
stretched, long seconds, and rather than let him gain the
impression she was desperately toadying up to him
Yancie said nothing more.

'So you concede,' he said at length, 'that the error
was yours yesterday, and not my keenness to "be the
centre of attention" in my Aston Martin?'

Did he *have* to bring that up? That niggle of anger
flickered again—and she realised, much though she
wanted to hang onto her job, that she had grovelled all
that she was going to. 'I've admitted I was totally in the
wrong,' she answered, unsmiling. To blazes with trying
to charm him—she guessed he lived on a diet of lemons
and vinegar.

He was as unimpressed by her unsmiling look as he
had been by her smiling one. 'I see you're wearing some
identification today.'

Which meant, she was positive, that he'd taken note
yesterday that she'd covered the firm's logo on her shirt
with a brooch. 'My name tag was on my jacket yesterday,' she replied pleasantly. Well, it had been—when
she'd been driving Mr Clements. 'My jacket was on the
passenger seat,' she explained.

She had thought he might keep on that theme, repri-
mand her for pinning the mother-of-pearl brooch over
the Addison Kirk logo on her shirt. But, to her surprise,
he left that particularly issue there, and commented instead, 'You've been with us a very short while,' and with

a straight, cold, no-nonsense kind of look asked, 'Do you enjoy your work, Miss Dawkins?'

It came as something of a relief not to have to lie or prevaricate—she had an idea that she wasn't very good at either. 'I love it,' she smiled.

She saw his glance flick from her eyes to her curving mouth, but he was as unreceptive to her charm as ever. 'Presumably you wish to keep your job?'

Yancie at once saw another glimmer of hope. By the sound of it he was more interested in giving her a grilling than dismissing her. 'I do,' she assured him sincerely.

'Why?' Just the one word.

Grilling? He was giving her a roasting! 'I've never done anything but housekeeping before,' she began to explain, by then certain that this very thorough man who knew she had been with the firm a very short while also knew that the previous occupation she'd listed on her application form was that of housekeeper. 'I thought I'd like a change. And I really love my work,' she smiled. She loved the freedom, the use of a car. 'I *am* a good driver,' she thought to mention. Though at his steady, grey-eyed stare she felt obliged to add, 'Normally.'

'You do appreciate that while you're wearing the company's uniform, and driving one of the company vehicles, that you are an ambassador for Addison Kirk?'

'Oh, yes,' she agreed, ready to agree to anything as the feeling started to grow that, by the skin of her teeth, it looked as if she might be able to hang onto her job.

'You also appreciate that any bad driving and subsequent insolence to another road user reflects extremely badly on the company?'

Oh, for Pete's sake! Yancie could feel herself getting annoyed again—what was it with this man? Quickly, she lowered her eyes. She couldn't afford to be annoyed. She couldn't afford that this shrewd man opposite should read in her eyes that she'd by far prefer to tell him to go take a running jump than answer him. She swallowed hard on her annoyance.

'Yes, I do appreciate that,' she replied as evenly as she could—and raised her eyes to see, astonishingly, the merest twitch at the right-hand corner of his mouth—for all the world as though she amused him!

In the next moment, however, his expression was as stern and as uncompromising as it had been throughout the interview. 'Good,' he said, and a wave of relief started to wash over Yancie. Surely that 'Good' must mean 'Right, you've had a wigging, now clear off and don't do it again'. She consequently got something of a shock when, his expression lightening very slightly, he stared fully and totally imperviously into her lovely blue eyes, and enquired, 'What were you doing on that stretch of the motorway yesterday?'

Crunch! With no little sense of disquiet, Yancie saw she had lost the tenuous hold she had on her job, as it suddenly went shooting from her grasp. And, because of it, her brain, usually lively and active, seemed to seize up. She should have been ready for this; but wasn't.

'I—er—I—er—paid for the petrol I used myself,' she heard herself say idiotically. 'I have authority to book petrol and oil to the company, but wh-when I stopped at that service station I paid...' Her voice trailed off at the realisation that—oh, you fool—she had just, by her statement, confirmed that she hadn't been on that stretch of the road on the firm's business.

Thomson Wakefield looked over to her, but if he was waiting to hear more he wasn't getting it. Her tongue, like her brain, had gone into reverse.

'That was very fair of you, Miss Dawkins—to pay for the petrol,' he commented silkily—but she suspected that sort of tone. And a second later knew she was right to suspect it when he continued, 'And the milometer? How did you square that?'

Like she was going to tell him! Like she was going to tell him any of the 'wrinkles' that went on down in the transport section! How, when Wilf Fisher had asked her to make that fifty-mile round trip on unofficial business, he'd said to give the correct mileage but, if asked why the extra mileage covered, to state that her passenger had asked her to do an errand. Either that, or the said passenger had asked her to take him to see a friend or family member. Since their passengers were almost exclusively board members or someone very high up in the executive tree, nobody, according to Wilf, would dream of questioning why the top brass had needed to do the extra mileage. Certainly, no one in the transport section.

'I'm waiting!'

Oh, crumbs! Dumbly Yancie stared at him. If he'd only smile—he had rather an attractive mouth. She blinked. *For goodness' sake pull yourself together*—had this man totally scrambled her brain?

'I—er—can't tell you,' she managed falteringly.

'What—the mileage scam or what you were doing being where you shouldn't have been?'

Neither, actually. 'There's no great scam,' she replied—well, you could hardly call fifty tiddly miles a scam.

'So, what business did you have—other than the company's business?'

Oh, honestly! Why didn't he back off? Because he was it, that was why. He was the numero uno, the big

cheese, and, having her on the end of his pin, he was
enjoying making her squirm—and she didn't like it. Had
her errand been for herself, then, she conceded, she
might very well have told him what she was about. But
there wasn't only herself to think about here—there was
Wilf. Wilf had a wife and four young children. And,
while Yancie was having to face that there was a very
real danger here that she might be looking for alternative
employment at any moment now, she just couldn't wish
the same fate on Wilf. She wouldn't be able to live with
herself if, through her, Wilf too was dismissed.

'You're not going to say?'

'I— No,' she mumbled.

Thomson Wakefield didn't seem to have expected any
other answer, but leaned back in his chair and, looking
sternly at her, he questioned, 'Just how badly do you
want to keep your job?'

Yancie felt sick in the pit of her stomach. She was
about to be dismissed, she knew it. 'Very badly,' she
answered. 'I really, really need it,' she emphasised, in a
last-ditch hope.

Thomson Wakefield's look sharpened. 'You have a
family to keep—a child?'

'I'm not married.'

He leaned back in his chair again, his look speculative. 'You are acquainted with the facts of life?' he queried.

Sarcastic pig; she didn't need him to tell her that you
could have a child without necessarily being married. 'I
know the theory,' she replied, putting in more effort to
stay calm. Though, at another of his long, steady stares,
she felt herself go a bit pink—and saw him take in her
blush, too. Well, it wasn't every day, or ever for that

matter, that she told a complete stranger that she was a virgin.

However, if her blush just now confirmed her statement for him, her ultimate employer did not comment on it either, but, with a quick glance to his watch, as if believing he had wasted more than enough of his precious time on her, Thomson Wakefield got to his feet. Yancie, too, was on her feet when at last he gave her the benefit of his deliberations.

'You may keep your job, Miss Dawkins,' he told her coldly.

'Oh, thank—'

'But…'

She might have known there'd be a 'But'. 'But?' she stayed to enquire.

'But you're suspended—without pay—until you give me an answer to my question of what you were doing on that part of the motorway.'

Thanks for nothing! Yancie came close then and there to telling him what he could do with his job. Why she didn't she couldn't have said. Her glance, however, was as cold as his when, just before she walked to the door, she told him coolly, 'I'll see myself out.'

It was Saturday morning before she had got herself of sufficient mind to begin thinking of something other than that cold and unfeeling brute Thomson Wakefield. Suspended! He might just as well have sacked her. No way could she bring Wilf into this. No point in both of them looking for a new job.

And that, she knew, had to be her first priority. She was still adamant that she wasn't going to touch a penny of the allowance which her stepfather paid into her bank account. But she had to face the fact that, even with

Astra refusing to allow her to pay rent, having been absolutely astounded at Yancie's suggestion that she
should, just day-to-day living was costly.

By Monday Yancie had double-read every likely job
in the situations vacant columns—there were not, she
had to face, very many for women without experience
in the workplace.

Though she knew in her heart of hearts that although,
as Thomson Wakefield had pointed out, she had been in
the job only a short while—and freedom aside—she felt
she really didn't want to work anywhere else but at the
Addison Kirk Group.

She supposed it must have something to do with the
people she worked with. Oh, not Thomson Wakefield;
she didn't care for him one tiny bit. If he was not exactly
the grumpy old devil she had told him he was, then it
couldn't be said either that he was full of the joys of
spring.

But the other people she worked with—other drivers,
Wilf, the executives she chauffeured around—to a man
they were all unfailingly pleasant. She thought of
Thomson Wakefield—she did quite often. And why
shouldn't she? She wouldn't have said he'd been unfailingly pleasant when he'd had the nerve to suspend
her. She had never driven him—the possibility that she
one day might didn't enter any equation. She'd better
carry on looking for another job.

It had been embarrassing returning to the transport
section after that loathsome interview with *him*. Had she
not left her shoulder bag in her locker Yancie felt she
might have made a hasty exit without anyone being any
the wiser.

Though, on reflection, she'd owed Kevin Veasey the
courtesy of telling him he was going to be a driver short,

if he didn't already know. Fortunately it had been after five when she'd made it back down to the transport section and most of the staff had left for the weekend.

'All right?' Kevin smiled as she approached, and Yancie knew then, from his manner, that apart from being extremely curious that she had been called to the top floor he had no earthly idea of why.

'Not exactly,' she replied, and, a little shamefaced, was obliged to admit, 'I've been suspended.'

'You've been...' Kevin stared at her in total surprise. 'Suspended!' he exclaimed. 'What for?'

'You don't know?' Clearly he didn't—Thomas Wakefield had not reported her to her department head, it seemed. But then, he didn't have to; he was handling it himself in his own beastly authoritarian way.

'I've no idea,' Kevin replied. 'I was instructed not to allow you to drive any of the vehicles today and for you to report to Mr Wakefield at four, but...'

'It's a long story,' Yancie said quietly.

'You don't want to tell me about it?'

Yancie shook her head. 'I'd better go home.'

'Keep in touch.'

She said she would, but couldn't see that she would. It was highly unlikely that Thomson Wakefield would relent and see Kevin was informed that her suspension was over.

Tuesday dawned cold and bleak and Yancie, who normally had a very sunny temperament, owned to feeling a bit out of sorts. She made a meal of duck with a cherry sauce for herself and her cousins, and hid her low spirits as, being excellent friends as well as cousins, they chatted about all and everything until Astra, the career-minded one of the three, said she was off to her study.

'And I'm off to try and make my peace with my mother,' Fennia sighed.

'That leaves me with the washing-up,' Yancie remarked—and they all laughed.

'Best of luck with your mother,' Yancie and Astra said in unison.

'I'll need it!'

Yancie was in the kitchen when, ten minutes later, the telephone rang. So as not to have Astra disturbed if she was in the middle of something deeply technical on her computer, Yancie went quickly to answer it. Should the call be for either her or Fennia, then there'd be no need for Astra to be interrupted.

'Hello, Yancie Dawkins,' said her cousin Greville cheerfully, instantly recognising her voice. 'How's the job going?'

Oh, heck, she had pondered long and hard on whether or not to tell her super half-cousin that she'd been suspended, but was still undecided. But now—it was decision time!

'Great!' she answered enthusiastically. How could she possibly confess that she had so dreadfully let him down? 'How are things with you? Still loving and leaving them?' Greville had been divorced for a number of years and, having been badly hurt, now, while having women friends, was careful to steer clear of emotional entanglements.

'Saucy monkey!'

She laughed. 'Did you want Astra? Fennia's out.'

'Any one of you,' he answered. 'I'm having a party on Saturday if all or any of you want to come.'

'We'd love to!' Yancie answered for the three of them. Greville threw wonderful parties.

They chatted for a few minutes more, and Yancie,

having managed to stay cheerful enough while talking
to him, felt immediately guilt-ridden once she had put
the phone down. She didn't like the feeling.

Fennia came home in low spirits too—her mother
hadn't wanted to know. Yancie did her best to cheer her,
telling her of Greville's phone call and party invite. 'Did
you tell him?'

'That I'm suspended? I couldn't.'

Astra came out of her study and, when Fennia volunteered to make some coffee, it was Astra who insisted
on making it.

All three of them went into the kitchen.

'Greville's having a party on Saturday—we're invited,' Yancie told her.

'Just what I could do with,' Astra declared. 'Thanks
for taking the call—I was up to my ears in complicated
calculations. Did you tell him?'

Yancie knew her cousin didn't mean had she accepted
for the three of them. 'I couldn't,' she admitted, and was
plagued all night when her guilty conscience kept her
awake. Greville had always been there for all three of
them—she owed it to him, after all he had done, to keep
her job.

Fennia's duty in going to try to put things right with
her mother reminded Yancie the next day—not that she
needed any reminding—that she had certain duties too.
And, though she didn't think of her stepfather as a duty,
she went, by public transport, to see him.

Her journey was extremely bothersome in that it involved a tube, a train and a bus. Though when her very
pleased-to-see-her stepfather said he wanted her to come
home and to forget about the car 'trouble', that he'd buy
her another one, Yancie found she could not accept.

'You're a darling,' she smiled, giving him a hug, 'but I couldn't.'

'Not even to make me happy?'

'Oh, don't!' she begged.

'I'm sorry,' he apologised at once. 'I never thought I'd resort to emotional blackmail. Come and tell me how your job's going. Your mother rang wanting to speak to you, by the way.'

'You didn't tell her I was working!'

'What—and get my ears chewed off for my trouble?' He chuckled. 'Coward though I am, I let her think you were still living here.' He thought for a moment, and then added, 'Have you seen her lately?'

'Not for a week or so,' Yancie replied.

But Ralph was patently anxious. 'What shall I say if she comes here looking for you?'

Yancie full well knew, her mother being a law unto herself, that she would turn up at her ex-husband's home if the idea occurred to her. 'I'll go and see her,' Yancie decided.

'Since you've obviously got the day off, you could go today,' Ralph Proctor hinted. 'You could take my car.'

Yancie looked at him and grinned. 'You're scared,' she teased. 'Scared she'll call.'

'Heaven alone knows where I got the nerve to ask her to marry me. Nor, when our marriage ended, found the nerve to insist you live with me.'

'You've got it when it counts,' Yancie told him softly.

She stayed and had lunch with him, his housekeeper seeming a very pleasant woman. And after lunch, his suggestion that Yancie borrow his car seeming a good one, she drove to her mother's imposing house some ten miles away to visit.

'You didn't ring to say you were coming!' Ursula

Proctor greeted her a shade peevishly. Yancie's mother was fifty-two but could easily have passed for ten years younger. She was beautiful still, so long as everything went her way. Today, on seeing her daughter unexpectedly, her mouth tightened expressively. 'I shall be able to spend fifteen minutes with you—I've an appointment with Henry. You should have phoned. I'm not here just waiting on the remote off-chance that you might drop by when the whim takes you, you know. And what are you doing with Ralph Proctor's car?'

Yancie guessed that Henry was probably her mother's hairdresser. After ten minutes with her, however, Yancie knew exactly why neither she nor her stepfather had mentioned to her parent that not only was she living elsewhere, but that for a few weeks she'd had a job. It was not so much cowardly as making for easier living. Her mother had the ability to carp endlessly about matters which other people took in their stride.

After returning her stepfather's car Yancie made her way back to Astra's apartment partly wishing that she hadn't left it that day. While her mother hadn't seemed particularly pleased to see her, her stepfather had. He wanted her to go back to live with him and for her to use the allowance he was still insisting on paying into her bank. But she couldn't. How could she possibly— how could she possibly return? It was just beyond her to touch a penny of his money after what Estelle had said.

Pride demanded she earn her own money from now on. The only problem with that was that she didn't have a job—and nothing she had seen in the situations vacant column which she was capable of doing was work that she wanted. Added to that, for all her stepfather had apologised for attempting emotional blackmail, Yancie was awash with guilt because she felt she couldn't go back to living in her old home with him. When she added all that guilt to how she had let Greville down after he had obtained that driver's job for her, Yancie's spirits sank even lower.

She owed it to Greville to try to hang onto her job. After his efforts on her behalf he didn't deserve that she should tell him—and soon knew she must—that she had been suspended. Suspended, too, not by her immediate boss but by none other than the top man himself!

She wanted that job, she truly did. Because the hours could be somewhat erratic, the job paid well. Oh, if only she wasn't' suspended! Oh, if only she had some other reason she could give other than she had gone fifty miles out of her way—leaving aside her cutting up the top of the top brass in the process—to deliver a spare kettle to Wilf Fisher's mother.

At dinner that night Fennia and Astra were interested in hearing about her day. Yancie told them of her visit to her stepfather, and, because Fennia was having difficulties with her mother, made light of the not very good reception she'd had from her own. And swiftly changed the conversation.

'How about your day?' she asked her cousin. 'Did all go well at the nursery?'

Fennia's reply was that they'd had a near disaster when one of the toddlers, who was inseparable from her fluffy elephant called Fanta, had mislaid it. 'Poor mite, she was inconsolable—she'd never have gone to sleep tonight without it.'

'But you did find it?'

Fennia's smile said it all. 'I was nearly in tears myself when Kate decided to inspect the backpack of one of our little trouble-makers.'

'And all was revealed?'

'He'd got his own soft toy—but he wanted Fanta.'

Yancie got up the following morning, said goodbye to her two cousins when they went off to work, and tried not to think of the notion which had come to her and which returned to pick at her again and again. It was unthinkable, she told herself—frequently.

And yet time, which had never previously hung heavily on her hands, was doing so now. Between them the cousins kept the apartment immaculate, so, having done what few chores there were, Yancie had plenty of time in which to wonder, Would it be so very wrong? And, for goodness' sake, who was she hurting?

No one, came the answer. The moment was born out of nowhere and before she knew it she was picking up the phone and dialling the Addison Kirk number.

'Veronica Taylor, please,' she requested firmly, when the phone was answered, and in next to no time she had Thomson Wakefield's PA on the line asking if she might help her. 'Oh, hello,' Yancie said cheerfully, while quite well aware that Veronica Taylor must know she'd been suspended, not prepared to flounder before she got started. 'My name's Yancie Dawkins; you may remember I saw Mr Wakefield last Friday—I wonder if I could have a word with him?'

'I'm afraid that's impossible.'

Drat! Yancie dug her heels in. Suddenly it was of paramount importance that she speak with the man that day. 'If he's in a meeting, perhaps you'd ask him to call me back,' she requested. Silence at the other end, and somehow Yancie gained the impression that men as busy as the boss of Addison Kirk were not noted for ringing the *hoi polloi* from the lowly transport section. That thought annoyed her—who the dickens did he think he was? She wasn't used to such treatment! 'Or, failing that, I'm free this afternoon; I could come in to see him,' she offered magnanimously. Since Yancie knew she was going to lie her head off, she would by far prefer to do it over the phone—if he was so busy, why waste his time seeing her personally?

'I'm afraid Mr Wakefield's time is fully booked today. If you'd like to hold on for a moment.' Yancie held on and a minute or so later the PA was back, and it soon transpired she had been to see the man himself when she said, 'If you'd care to look in tomorrow, say around midday, Mr Wakefield will try and slot you into his busy schedule.'

'I should be prepared to wait?' *Should I bring sandwiches?*

'Mr Wakefield is an exceptionally busy man,' Veronica Taylor answered pleasantly.

So why didn't he just pick up his phone now? It was ridiculous that she should have to go and sit there and, remembering the last time, wait and wait. He was in his office so why didn't he just pick up his perishing phone and let her get her lies said, done and over with now? But, Yancie reminded herself, she wanted her job back; she truly, truly did. And if this was what she had to do to get it, so be it. 'I'll be in tomorrow—around midday, as you suggest,' she said nicely, adding a polite goodbye—and realised that yet again, without even having spoken with him, Thomson Wakefield had managed to disturb her equilibrium.

When she had calmed down from her niggle of annoyance, Yancie started to feel quite excited about her interview tomorrow. So much depended on its outcome. And truly she was a good driver. She'd made a mistake, but she'd learned from it, and if only Thomson Wakefield would give her another chance... Now, what should she wear?

She had a wardrobe or two full of really wonderful clothes. Somehow, when she had never felt the need of a confidence boost before, Yancie now experienced the oddest desire to want to look her very, very best when she saw Thomson Wakefield tomorrow.

Which, she scoffed a minute or so later, was just so much nonsense—no man had the right to tilt her confidence a little, or even the merest fraction. She went and checked out a fresh uniform.

At eleven fifty-five the following morning Yancie, suited in her newly dry-cleaned uniform and crisp beige shirt, presented herself at Veronica Taylor's office. Yancie had debated whether or not to wear her name tag, but thought, since Thomson Wakefield knew perfectly well who she was, that she wouldn't bother. She had, in fact, been halfway out the door of the apartment when it had dawned on her that for someone desperate to be reinstated she was risking it.

So now, duly labelled, she sat in Veronica Taylor's office while the PA rang through to the next-door office to inform her boss—their boss, with any luck—that Yancie Dawkins was there.

Anticipating that the great man would squeeze her into his busy schedule about two minutes before he went for his lunch around one, Yancie had barely read five pages of her book before he buzzed through to say he would see her now.

Yancie, wishing she'd spent her waiting time re-rehearsing the tale she was about to tell, quickly put her paperback in her shoulder bag and, feeling oddly nervous—which was totally absurd, she told herself—she went to the other door in the room, knocked briefly, and went in.

Thomson Wakefield was just as she remembered him. Today he wore a dark suit, striped shirt and, as he rose from his chair to indicate she should take the seat she had used a week ago, she saw he was as tall, and as nearly good-looking, as ever.

'Good morning,' she broke the silence that emanated from the non-talkative brute. 'Er, afternoon,' she corrected, crossing to the chair—not a glimmer of a smile! Here we go—it was like treading through sticky treacle. 'Thank you for seeing me at such short notice,' she heard herself say—creepy or what?

Yancie clamped her lips shut, and took the seat he offered; only the ever present knowledge of how much she wanted this job—nay, *needed* this job—prevented her from getting up and marching out again.

She looked at him. His glance flicked over her. If he observed her name tag neatly in place—and from the little she knew of him she suspected he missed little— he did not comment. In fact he said nothing at all for a good few seconds, but unsmilingly took in her neatly brushed shoulder-length ash-blonde hair and complexion—once rated by some male as exquisite. Wakefield was totally unaffected.

When he did speak, it was to remind her, 'You wished to see me?'

So he was throwing the ball into her court. She took a deep breath—bother the man for making her nervous. 'I want my job back,' she said bluntly—oh, grief, she hadn't rehearsed it this way. She saw a trace of ice chill his eyes, and guessed she wasn't going the right way to get it. 'Please,' she added, as an afterthought.

Last Friday, in this room, she had thought—very

briefly—that the man opposite had marginally cracked
his face a touch, as if she'd amused him. His mouth
tweaked again, but it was so fleeting, she was again certain she was mistaken. In any case, she didn't care to be
laughed at.

'So?' he enquired curtly.

So? She stared at him from puzzled and deeply blue
eyes. 'Oh!' It suddenly clicked.

Though before she could get her wits together and
rush into her story Thomson Wakefield, as if thinking
her particularly dense, enlightened her. 'So why should
I give you your job back?'

Yancie didn't care to be thought dense either. 'Because I need it,' she answered, which she realised was
not the answer he wanted. Therefore, before she started
to lie her head off, she managed to find a smile, which
had much the same effect on him as any of her other
smiles—precisely none—and bucked her ideas up. 'Obviously you want to know what I was doing driving
where I shouldn't have been a week ago last Thursday,'
she said prettily.

He was unimpressed, but his glance to his watch, as
if to say if she didn't soon spit it out he'd be making
that suspension permanent, prodded her to get on with
it. 'It might be an idea,' he suggested, and Yancie was
certain she heard sarcasm there.

It was the annoyance she felt with him, his sarcasm,
and his barely concealed impatience that he could look
at his watch, which gave her the kick start she needed.
'I really can't think why I didn't tell you the truth before,' she lied. 'Other than, of course, I knew I was in
the wrong, and...' she tried another smile—zilch! '...no-
body likes to be in the wrong.' Silence. 'But, the plain
truth of the matter is, I went to see my sister.'

'Your sister?'

She might well have said 'cousin' since she did have those, but had no sister. But Yancie was ever conscious of her connection with her board member half-cousin, Greville, and, fearing she might trip herself up if she started talking 'cousins', she'd thought it better to invent a sister. In her view if she was going to have to tell a lie anyway she might as well make it a good one.

'My sister had been to stay with me for a few days, with her toddler daughter—er—Miranda. Anyhow,' Yancie rushed on, suddenly starting to feel extremely uncomfortable at lying—though still feeling unable to tell the truth and bring Wilf into it. 'Anyhow, my n-niece has this soft toy, a lion, called Leo. She's devoted to Leo, but no sooner had they arrived back at their home, early, very early on Thursday morning, than my sister was ringing me to say they'd just discovered Miranda had left Leo behind, and was inconsolable without him.' Yancie, most of her lying out of the way, looked directly at Thomson Wakefield. She smiled; he didn't. 'You know how children are.'

He surveyed her coolly. 'I don't have any.'

'Well—er—I'm sure your wife would know...'

'Had I a wife, Miss Dawkins, I'm sure she would, but I am not married.'

'Oh!' Yancie looked at him with fresh eyes. Given that his smiles were non-existent, to anybody who didn't dislike him as much as she did, she supposed he *was* good-looking—in fact, quite dishy.

'Oh?' he queried when she had added nothing.

Yancie quickly got herself back together again. Dishy? Was she crazy? 'Oh, anyway, the child—er—Miranda wouldn't have slept a wink that Thursday night if I hadn't been able to get Fanta—I mean Leo—to her.

As I mentioned, she was already fretting dreadfully. I promised my sister I'd get the—er—lion to her that day. But—how?'

His grey eyes were cool. In fact, as he looked steadily at her, the whole of the man seemed cool; while suddenly she was boiling hot—well, who wouldn't be after trotting out that load of balderdash? But, balderdash or not, had he believed it?

Yancie waited, barely breathing, and was so relieved she didn't have a chance to feel guilty when it seemed he had, indeed, believed her, when he stated, 'You decided to deliver the—lion—personally.'

'I know I shouldn't have, and I wouldn't do such a thing again,' she promised. 'But it was an emergency, and little Cassandra's—M-Miranda—she's sometimes called Cassandra...' *clown, concentrate* '...stopped crying the moment she saw her adored lion.'

'For which we must all be truly grateful,' Thomson Wakefield commented dryly. Sarcastic devil. Yancie waited, wondering if she had said too little, but afraid to say more. This lie-telling wasn't as easy as she'd imagined. She waited, stumped to know anyhow what more she could say. Then the head man was leaning back in his chair. 'So you think, on the strength of what you've just told me, I should consider cancelling your suspension?'

'If you wouldn't mind,' she requested quietly.

And had to bear his long scrutiny before Thomson Wakefield said, 'Very well.' Hope rose—but she'd thought she'd still got her job last Friday—until he'd added that 'but'.

'You mean, I'm reinstated?' she checked carefully.

'As of now,' he confirmed. 'Though, after you've been to see Kevin Veasey, I suggest you go home.'

Yancie stared at him, her confusion showing. 'I'm re-instated, but I'm to go home? I don't understand.'

'You're driving tomorrow,' he enlightened her. 'Any problem with that?'

Tomorrow was Saturday, but… 'Not one,' she quickly assured him.

'Good.'

'I expect Kevin will tell me who I'm driving, and where,' she remarked, relief starting to enter her soul—she had her job back, she did, she did! The interview was over—and she'd been reinstated!

But before she could politely thank Thomson Wakefield for allowing her to continue to work for the firm, prior to getting to her feet and getting out of there, he was knocking them straight from under her by saying smoothly, 'Oh, I can tell you that.' And with something near to a smile on his face he announced, 'You'll be driving me.'

Yancie stared at him, and blushed, though she had not the smallest notion why she should blush—something emotional, she supposed. 'You!' she said faintly—this the man last seen driving himself in an Aston Martin!

'Strange though it seems to you,' he replied, a man who apparently was able to add mind-reader to the rest of his accomplishments, 'I quite often require to be driven to some meeting or other.'

He had meetings, on a Saturday! On reflection, Yancie supposed that he would. Thinking about it, she realised that no business was likely to so much as get off the ground, much less be the giant concern Addison Kirk was, if those at the top, the decision-makers, shut up shop on the dot of five every Friday evening.

'Yes, of course,' she agreed—well, she wasn't likely to start disagreeing with him, not now—not now she had

her lovely job back. 'If—er—you can give me some
loose idea of the time your meeting is scheduled to fin-
ish,' she went on agreeably, adding hurriedly, 'I know,
of course, that meetings very often overrun—which, naturally, isn't a problem; I'll still be in ample time to attend Gr...the party I'm going to tomorrow night.'
Yancie started to feel hot all over again because she had
almost slipped up there and mentioned Greville's name,
even though she knew there was more than one male
with the name Greville out there.

But Thomson Wakefield was nearly smiling again,
and didn't look in the least tiny bit sorry when he went
on to let her know that her surmise that his meeting was
a morning one was totally erroneous. 'I'm afraid you'll
be missing your party tomorrow evening,' he informed
her smoothly.

Her blue eyes widened. 'I will?'

'Weren't you advised at your job interview that, as
well as the work sometimes involving erratic hours,
there would occasionally be times when you'd be required to stay away from home overnight?'

Yancie stared blankly at him. She was going to have
to go away with her least favourite person, and stay
away overnight!

'Y-yes,' she stammered, pulling herself together.

'You do *still* want the job?'

Yancie started to hate him—and his threats. 'Of
course.' The actress awoke in her, and she smiled. 'Not
a problem. May I ask where we're going? I'd like to
look at a road map.'

He stood up, the interview over. 'Mrs Taylor will give
you all the details.'

Yancie stood up too. 'Do I need to...?' She broke off
as it came to her that he would not countenance having

a PA who was anything other than *par excellence*. 'I
expect Mrs Taylor will attend to my overnight accom-
modation.'

He walked with her to the interconnecting door. 'You
catch on fast,' he said.

Very fast, she would have said. She had been going
to thank him for reinstating her. But all at once she was
on to realising that, as he wouldn't suffer a PA who
wasn't *par excellence*, neither would he suffer having
someone drive him who wasn't of the same quality.

And Yancie knew then—forget his magnanimity in
reinstating her. What tomorrow was about was Thomson
Wakefield checking at first hand the quality of her driving skills. If she didn't measure up, he would no doubt
be telling her, within a very few miles, *Reinstatement?
Forget it; you're out*.

To think she had been going to thank him! *He* could
forget that, for a start!

CHAPTER THREE

YANCIE was up extra early the next morning. She was due to pick up her passenger at eight sharp. There was absolutely no way she was going to be late. Thomson Wakefield wanted to judge how good she was—she intended to show him, in all respects. She was going to be on time, smart and courteous and, above all, ensure that he would find no fault with her driving.

Fortunately, her cousins were early risers too, and Astra, scheduled to meet a client later, volunteered to give her a lift to Addison Kirk where Yancie would pick up the Jaguar prior to collecting her boss. Then she would head up the motorway with Thomson Wakefield to a conference on the other side of Leeds.

'A pity you'll miss Greville's party tonight,' Astra commented as they drove, knowing Yancie had telephoned him last night to say she wouldn't be able to make it because she was driving Thomson Wakefield north.

'You more than anyone know that work comes before pleasure,' Yancie answered. 'Do you never get tired of it?'

'Not so far,' Astra grinned, and soon they were chatting away about work, finance and about Yancie's journey when Astra suddenly remembered, 'Doesn't Charlie Merrett live up that way?'

'He does!' Yancie too remembered. 'He liked it so much, he stayed up there when he finished university.' The three cousins and Charlie had been at nursery school together. He had been a shy, diffident boy, and between them, as young as they'd been, the three girls had started mothering him. They still, if spasmodically, kept in touch. 'Enjoy the party,' Yancie smiled as she got out of the car at Addison Kirk.

'Show him how brilliant you are,' Astra smiled back, having heard her cousin's theory that if she didn't perform well that day she knew it would be bye-bye time.

The Jaguar was a wonderful car to drive. Black in colour, sleek in its lines, little or no effort was required to have it purring along.

Thomson Wakefield lived about an hour's journey away from the office, and it had just gone seven-thirty when, as smart as new paint in her uniform, Yancie turned up the sweeping drive to his elegant rural Georgian home.

Because she was early, Yancie opted to wait in the car until just a few minutes before eight. She had only been sitting there for a short while, however, when the front door of the house opened, and a suited Thomson Wakefield came out.

Yancie left the car and had a bright, but courteous 'Good morning' hovering on her lips—but it was totally not needed. 'You can't sit out here in the cold for half an hour,' her employer clipped before she could say a word. 'You'd better come into the house.'

Chivalry was not dead, then! 'I...' she opened her mouth to argue that, yes, she could, that the car was lovely and warm, then realised that to argue wasn't the way smart and courteous went.

'Good morning,' she said anyway, and was left, unanswered, to trail after him into his lovely home.

'Go and find my housekeeper and get her to make you

a cup of coffee,' he decreed, pointing Yancie down a long and wide hall.

Yancie didn't want a cup of coffee. She opened her mouth to say as much, to refuse his invitation. Then supposed she had a lot to learn about this work environment business—it wasn't an invitation, but an order.

She started down the hall; he crossed it to what she could see from the open door was a study. Another door was open further down the hall; she saw it was a drawing room, and went in. She'd wait there.

Yancie was staring out of one of the long windows—for all it was a murky wet morning, she could not help but admire the peace and tranquillity of the setting—when Thomson Wakefield, briefcase under one arm, an overnight bag in his hand, came into the room.

She turned at the small sound, and, feeling suddenly her old sunny self, but attributing it to the restfulness of his home, she gave him the benefit of her natural smile. 'It's lovely here,' she said without thinking, and for a moment thought, as he stared at her, that he was about to smile back. Perish the thought.

He glanced down to the small table which wasn't littered with a coffee cup. 'We'll go,' he unsmilingly announced.

Yancie's sunny side went into hiding. She went out to the car with him, enquiring politely, 'Shall I take your bag for you?' when they reached the boot of the car, and found herself surplus to requirements when he opened the boot himself and dropped down his expensive-looking overnight bag next to her expensive-looking overnight bag.

Still trying to get it right, Yancie dutifully had the rear passenger door open for him when, boot lid closed, he walked round the side of the car. Without so much as a glance to her, he tossed in his briefcase and then got in. Yancie civilly closed the door, and went up front to the driver's seat.

She owned, as she drove along—carefully and solicitously to other road users—that, whereas with other executives she would very soon forget she was carrying a passenger at all, somehow, she couldn't forget about Thomson Wakefield in the back.

And why would she forget him? Didn't she have to be on her toes today where he was concerned? No way did she want this weekend's work to end with laughing-Jack back there giving her the big heave-ho.

Yancie took a glance in her mirror, not at the road behind, but at him. Their eyes met! Her tummy did the most peculiar somersault. Quickly, she looked away. 'Er—would you like the heating turned up—er—or down?' she enquired, purely from a sudden need, never before known, to say something.

'No,' he answered briefly.

Suit yourself! Yancie carried on driving, and a short while later realised Thomson Wakefield was not gripping onto the leatherwork for dear life—as she'd supposed he might—but had so far forgotten his driver, he was getting on with some work. Surely that meant he was comfortable with her driving! Yancie, while alert to the rainy road conditions, started to otherwise relax.

An hour and a half later and he was still hard at work. If he wasn't reading reports and making notes, he was making calls on the car phone, or dictating material for Veronica Taylor to type back. Did the man never rest?

'We'll stop at the next service station,' she heard him say, and for a moment she thought he was still dictating a letter.

When the service station was duly reached, however,

and Yancie decided to stay in the car and wait for him, Thomson Wakefield came round to her door and opened it for her to step out.

'I don't want...' she began.

And got the shock of her life when he said curtly, 'You need a break,' and she realised that the stop was for her benefit. To realise he wasn't risking her getting eye-strain or overtired in the wet weather.

'You're right, of course,' she murmured, pleasantly, and stepped out of the car—but, as he blocked her way, found she wasn't going anywhere for a moment or two.

'Take your name tag off,' he instructed.

She blinked—she had been told to wear it at all times. 'My name tag?' she enquired witlessly—what was it about this man? Usually she had a brain.

'Take it off,' he repeated, with more patience than she would have given him credit for. 'I know you're trying hard—but I've a feeling you'd prefer not to let all and sundry know that you're Yancie Dawkins from Addison Kirk.'

'Well, not unless we've been formally introduced,' she said with a smile, saw his glance flick to her up-turned mouth—but he didn't smile.

It was uphill all the way with this one, she mused, as himself, not needing a break, apparently, sent her off to get a coffee, then went back to his telephoning. And yet it had been thoughtful of him. And what about the way her insides had somersaulted when her eyes had met his in the rear-view mirror? Something very peculiar was going on here!

Yancie returned to the car after a fifteen-minute break, denying that anything in any way peculiar was going on. The only reason her tummy had been a bit butterfly-like was because it was so vitally important that she did her job well that day.

On his instruction she drove straight to the conference centre, and when he got out of the car she got out of the car too. 'I shall be some hours here,' he stated. Ho-hum—more hanging about! But not so, apparently, she discovered, when, standing there and looking down at her, he went on, 'You've got the name and address of our hotel; go and book us both in—perhaps you wouldn't mind having my bag put in my room.' Perhaps you *wouldn't mind!* 'Then go and have some lunch. I'll see you back here at five-thirty.'

She didn't have to hang about waiting! He was giving her time off! For good behaviour? Yancie's natural smile came out. 'Have a good conference,' she bade him, before she could stop to consider—were mere drivers supposed to say things like that?

The hotel, when she found it, was large, expensive, and efficient. Having expected, however, that she would be shut away in a broom cupboard somewhere, Yancie was agreeably surprised to find Veronica Taylor had booked her a room of the same quality as their employer's. Yancie knew this because, wanting to ensure that nothing went wrong this weekend while she was being 'put through her paces', she went personally with the bell-boy up to the floor above hers to deposit Thomson Wakefield's bag.

She then realised that she was hungry and so went down to the hotel's restaurant and enjoyed a leisurely lunch. Presumably lunch was laid on for her employer at the conference centre. Back in her room she unpacked her bag, shaking out the folds of the dress she had brought with her, and also the trousers and shirt. She hadn't done an overnight job before, but unless she had to she wasn't minded to stay in her uniform the whole time.

She freshened her make-up, brushed her pale hair and decided against changing into a new shirt. She'd brought two with her, but, needing one to go home in tomorrow, she might need a fresh one to wear tonight should he require her to chauffeur him to some other meeting. What did she know? Heads of companies might have meetings every Saturday night for all she knew.

Wanting to be in plenty of time, Yancie was at the conference hall with a half-hour to spare. Perhaps they'd finished early—perhaps they were overrunning—she went inside to find out.

There seemed to be no one about so Yancie nosed about. When she came to some double doors she thought they looked interesting and she opened one of them. She found herself standing at the back of a crowded hall, where, apart from the man now on the platform speaking, there was otherwise a silence in which you could have heard the proverbial pin drop. The man now speaking was none other than the man she had come to collect. Thomson Wakefield.

Not wanting to draw attention to herself by going out again, Yancie spotted one chair at the back that was vacant and silently crossed to it, and sat down. She listened to what he was saying. Truly Thomson Wakefield had a wonderful voice. She looked carefully about—and could not help but be taken with the way he held his audience. She felt quite proud suddenly—and wasn't sure that her heart didn't give a little flutter.

Totally absurd, of course, and yet… She listened—my word, did he know his subject! He was quite spellbinding. No wonder he headed Addison Kirk. A burst of applause erupted, and then someone was closing the conference.

When people started getting to their feet, so too did Yancie. She was the first out and by the time her employer came out from the building she was sitting primly behind the steering wheel. He was not alone but was in conversation with several other men before, with handshakes all round, he headed over to where she was parked.

It was still a cold, damp day. She considered, as befitted her position in life, getting out and opening the passenger door for him, but, on balance, decided that he was quite big enough to open the door for himself.

He got in. If he'd seen her enter the conference hall—and quite honestly, for all he hadn't faltered in his speech, she couldn't see how he might have missed seeing her—he didn't comment on it. In fact he had nothing at all to say.

Which left her to slew round in her seat, and enquire, 'To the hotel?'

He nodded and, terrific orator though he might be, Yancie, steering away from the pavement, started to feel a bit peeved that he had so few words for her. Peeved? Good grief, she was out to show him what a good, polite, thoughtful, absolutely terrific employee she was. She didn't have space to be peeved this trip!

Having given herself a small talking-to, Yancie started to lighten up, and as they left a built-up area behind she looked in her mirror—and again discovered his glance on her. Their eyes met, and Yancie found herself saying, 'That was some speech you made!'

His eyes widened the merest fraction, though not from surprise that she had been in that hall, she was sure, but more from the fact that she'd referred to it—either that, or surprise that she was dishing out a compliment.

'You know anything at all about ergonomics?' he enquired, his tone cool.

'Not the first thing,' Yancie owned, and laughed—he didn't. She was getting just a trifle fed up with him. 'Perhaps that's why I'm so easily impressed,' she added, and was scowled at for her trouble.

'Watch your driving!' he instructed her shortly, and Yancie began to wonder if she would ever get the hang of this being employed business.

While she was certain that few went around being servile these days, she was having one heck of a time in remembering that she was a driver and, therefore, while at work, not an equal. Thomson Wakefield was the top man and she a mere driver, and she'd better remember that.

Yancie was of the view that the journey to the hotel would be completed without him saying another word to her. She was mistaken. She had just driven into a semi-rural area near to the hotel when the car phone rang—she left it to her employer to pick it up. Quite obviously, since he used the vehicle as an extension of his office, the call was for him. Besides which, no one of her acquaintance knew this telephone number.

Or so she thought. She heard him answer the phone— then nearly jumped in surprise when he said shortly, 'For you.'

She half turned in her seat. *'For me?'* she asked half-wittedly, one hand leaving the steering wheel as if to take the phone from him.

'Pull over!' he ordered.

Yancie pulled over onto a grass verge, her mind going from stunned to racing. It had to be Kevin Veasey; he

was working all day today. It had gone six, but he often
worked late. Perhaps some urgent job for tomorrow had
come up and he wanted her to go somewhere once she'd
dropped off her present passenger.

With the car halted, she turned and took the phone
from her employer. 'Hello?' she said—and just couldn't
believe the voice she heard—it was not Kevin Veasey.

'Who was that?' her mother demanded of the man
who had answered the phone.

'What's wrong?' Yancie asked quickly, stunned but
realising her mother would only have traced her to this
number in an emergency.

She should, she almost at once acknowledged, have
known her mother better than that. 'Nothing's wrong!'
her mother retorted tartly. 'Everything couldn't be more
right. Who was that who answered the phone?' she repeated.

'Er—nobody you know,' Yancie managed, getting
herself a little together; though heartily glad she had her
back to Thomson Wakefield, she had an idea she was a
pretty shade of scarlet.

'Are you going steady with someone?' Ursula Proctor
demanded.

'Mother!'

'I don't know what's the matter with you! When I
was your age I had men cutting a path to my door.
You're pretty. If I do say it myself, you're quite beautiful
sometimes. Why...'

'I'm—er—a little busy right now.'

'I've spent the best part of today trying to contact
you—and now you haven't time to talk to me.' Her
mother broke off to draw breath. 'You'd better come
over and see me—I'll expect you tonight at...'

'I can't come tonight.'

'Why ever not?'

Oh, grief, there seemed no way she was going to be able to get her mother off the line until she was ready to go—and Yancie was in agonies, knowing that Wakefield esquire was tuned in to every answer she made. 'I'm not at home this weekend.'

'You've never gone away with some man?'

'I'll ring you later...' Yancie began.

'No, you won't. Ralph said you were out for the day, but when I rang Delia to tell her my news Greville answered the phone, so I told him—and mentioned at the same time the problem I was having getting hold of you.' Poor Greville! Her mother was still giving forth, taking her to task for giving her half-cousin her car phone number and not her, when Yancie blanked off, her thoughts on her cousin. Poor Greville; the fact of her mother 'mentioning' anything meant that her mother had gone on at him ad infinitum. Yancie then knew that Greville, probably meaning only to nip into Aunt Delia's to collect something or other she had prepared for his party that night, had been delayed by her mother bending his ear for half an hour. Yancie guessed he probably had a note of the firm's car phone numbers in his wallet, and must have given her mother this phone number from sheer, worn-down desperation.

'What was your news?' Yancie questioned when her mother broke off to draw another breath, realising only too well that, short of unforgivably putting the phone down on her mother, she wasn't going to be able to end this conversation until she heard it.

'I'm getting married again!' her mother announced bluntly. 'Naturally, I wanted you to be the first to know.'

'Oh, I'm sorry.' Yancie was instantly apologetic.

'I'd have preferred your congratulations!' her mother retorted acidly.

'Well, of course, I'm pleased for you. I...'

'Good, you can come and meet Henry tomorrow,' her mother snorted pithily—and hung up. And Yancie felt as if she'd just been pulled through the wringer.

Absently she handed the phone back to Thomson, and only realised that she had forgotten that he was breathing down her neck for all of two seconds when, mildly for him, he enquired, 'Family problems?'

In an instant Yancie was back to realising she was in a car parked on a grass verge, not chauffeuring the man she was hoping to impress with her efficiency. 'I'm sorry,' she apologised. 'My mother's—er—um—just got engaged.' Yancie started to feel hot all over. 'She— um—wanted me to be the first to know,' she explained, and set the car in motion, hoping with all she had that her employer would think the news qualified as suffi- ciently urgent for her mother to have contacted her through the garage, via Kevin Veasey, who had passed on the car's phone number to her.

Not another word was said, and by the time she had driven onto the forecourt of the hotel Yancie was giving serious thought to telling her mother when next she saw her—tomorrow or die, by the sound of it—that she was not only no longer living at Ralph's home, but that she had found herself a job. Well, to be more exact, Greville had found her a job.

Yancie took a swift glance at Thomson Wakefield as they got out of the car. *If* she still had a job, that was. His glance at her was brief, then he was striding towards the hotel entrance. She went hurrying with him and started to feel annoyed. She half expected when they reached the door of the hotel and he opened it that he would go through and leave it to swing back in her face. But no, he did have some manners, it seemed, in that he held it open for her to go through first.

They were at Reception waiting for their keys when he informed her that he would not be requiring her services that evening. 'I'm dining with some people I'm doing some business with. I see no point in you waiting around or coming to collect me when I've no idea what time I shall need you.'

'You'd like the car keys?'

'I'll take a taxi.'

That probably meant he was celebrating some business deal with a glass or two of something! 'If you're sure?' she checked—this to a man she was growing positive was sure in all he did.

He didn't deign to answer, and they were going up to their rooms in the lift when he told her, 'Make certain you have something to eat yourself.' Yancie got out of the lift on her floor and *she* didn't deign to answer.

She was in her room when she began to wonder why the man had the power to—without effort—niggle her so. Probably, she pondered, because she had never met a man like him before. The man was an automaton. 'Make certain you have something to eat yourself,' he'd said. Well, of course, she would.

Though, having eaten in the hotel's dining room by herself at lunchtime, she had little wish to dine by herself that night. But the only person she knew in this neck of the woods was Thomson Wakefield, and he was dining elsewhere, thank you very much.

She paused then and stood stock-still as the thought suddenly came to her—was that why she was feeling all niggled? Because he hadn't asked her to dine with him? Oh, *come on*! As if she wanted to dine with him, for

goodness' sake! To do so would mean she was keen for
his company, that she liked him. Why, she couldn't even
stand the man!

Having indisputably established that fact, Yancie did a
mental trawl of girls she'd been at boarding-school with,
but, before she could come up with a name, she remembered Charlie Merrett. She reached for the phone.

'Fennia,' she said when her cousin answered, 'have
we got Charlie Merrett's phone number between us?'

Fennia had it in her address book, and not only gave
it to her but said Greville had phoned to say if Yancie
got in touch and said her mother had found her would
she forgive him? 'Apparently Aunt Ursula was particularly hell-bent on finding you,' Fennia added.

Yancie had a ten-minute conversation with her cousin
and told her to tell their half-cousin that she understood
perfectly; that she'd probably have done the same in
similar circumstances, and that she forgave him completely.

After her phone call to Fennia, Yancie rang Charles
Merrett's number. *'Yancie!'* he exclaimed when he heard
her. 'How're things going? Lovely to hear from you.
Still in London?'

'At this moment, I'm nearer to you than I am to
London. You're not free to have dinner, are you?'

'Am I not!' he answered eagerly. 'Just give me a minute to cancel my arrangements for tonight, and I'll be
with you.'

'Oh, I wouldn't want you to cancel...'

'*I* would! I can see my male friends any old time,' he
said warmly.

'You're sure?'

'Where are you?'

Because it seemed she was staying in a hotel in an

opposite direction from where Charlie lived, Yancie said she'd make her own way to the restaurant he'd suggested.

'I couldn't let you,' he argued.

'Yes, you could,' she laughed, and had only one other question to ask before she agreed to meet him at the appointed place at eight-thirty. 'Does this restaurant have a car park?'

'That's a small part of the reason why it's so popular,' he answered.

Yancie took a shower feeling pleased, since it sounded as if the restaurant they were going to was very upmarket, that she had brought the dress with her that she had. After her shower, she dressed her white-blonde hair in a knot on top of her head, applied the small amount of make-up she normally wore, and slipped into the long-sleeved ankle-length black lace dress with its black silk petticoat lining.

She left her room knowing that she looked good and, strangely, half wishing that Thomson Wakefield could see her. Well, she defended, when trying to work out why she should think anything so ridiculous, she wouldn't have said her brown uniform was the most flattering garment she had ever owned—but it was the only thing he had ever seen her in—or was likely to, for that matter.

Yancie had a small, but only a very small, tussle with her conscience on whether she, like her employer, should take a taxi. But why, for goodness' sake? She had a perfectly good car out there doing nothing, and she knew that she wouldn't have any trouble parking it. It wasn't as if she was likely to bump into Thomson Wakefield or anything like that, was she? Nor, since he'd taken a taxi, which indicated he intended to do a little celebrating, was it likely that he'd be back before she was.

Charlie Merrett was just as she remembered him from the last time she'd seen him—about a year ago. Tall, handsome and around the same age as Yancie, she found him as willing and eager to please as ever he had been.

'You're gorgeous, Yancie. Absolutely gorgeous,' he said enthusiastically as they entered the restaurant.

Who wouldn't be fond of him? 'And so are you,' she teased him, and they both laughed. Then, as the head waiter came up to them, so Yancie looked about—and nearly went into heart failure. There, across the room, wining and dining at a table with several other people, sat Thomson Wakefield. And, while he was looking straight at her, at the same time he managed to look straight through her.

Oh, crumbs. While he wasn't acknowledging her, Yancie knew he had registered her. Too late now to wish she'd taken a taxi—oh, help—she had the firm's car out there. A car, she swiftly realised, which, since Thomson Wakefield had already started on his meal, he was bound to see when, as was likely, he left the restaurant before she did!

It fleetingly crossed her mind to pop outside and park the car somewhere else. But that was just a thought in the panic of the moment. For heaven's sake, hadn't he said—no, ordered her—to have something to eat? Well, that was exactly what she was doing—obeying orders. He hadn't specified where she should eat, had he?

Yancie was profoundly thankful just the same that the waiter led her and Charlie to a table in a small alcove. At least she was spared having to look at the boss man while she ate. Though that too bothered her because, being unable to see him, she started to feel all on edge that any moment she would feel a hand on her shoulder and hear a cold voice request that she hand over the car keys.

She pushed Thomson Wakefield out of her head and made herself concentrate on Charlie Merrett. She had asked him out to dinner, so the least she could do was to play the game. Though in truth Charlie seemed happy enough just to be there.

'So what have you been doing?' she asked, and the next hour went by with the two of them catching up on the happenings of the last twelve months.

Yancie discovered that, while finding it impossible to lie to a friend, she was avoiding telling Charlie that she had left home and had a job—even though it was highly unlikely that he would bump into her mother and comment on it.

They were tucking into a fine pudding when Charlie looked across the table and suddenly recalled, 'You never said what you were doing in my part of the world.'

Yancie took a spoonful of the fruit and meringue concoction while she thought how best to answer. 'Someone I know was giving a speech at a conference centre up this way,' she smiled. 'It was quite something.'

'That sort of thing—making a speech—would terrify me,' he said. 'Is your pudding all right?' No wonder they were all so fond of Charlie.

It was about half past ten, when they had drunk the last of their coffee, that Yancie told Charlie how super it was to see him again but that she'd been up early that morning and thought she'd go back to her hotel and her bed.

'You'll give my love to Fennia and Astra,' he beamed, and as Yancie promised she would she was bracing herself to walk through the restaurant where *he* was dining.

Should she give him a smile or, following his example, do a bit of looking straight through him?

It irritated her that this man should do this to her confidence and make her so that she had to *think* how to act rather than follow her natural instincts. However, the situation of whether to smile or whether to look straight through Thomson Wakefield didn't arrive because, when she took a glance over to where he had been sitting, she saw that he wasn't there. His party had gone.

She and Charlie hugged and kissed farewell in a friendly fashion, knowing, without pain, that it could be another twelve months before they saw each other again, and Yancie began her journey back to the hotel.

She'd had an extremely pleasant evening with Charlie Merrett, but it was not thoughts of Charlie that occupied her on that drive—but Thomson Wakefield. Had he gone back to the hotel—had he gone on somewhere?

Gone on somewhere, she decided. Grief, it was only a little after half past ten. On a Saturday night, too! Of course, his dinner had been of the business variety, but corporate entertaining—she was sure she'd heard that phrase somewhere—didn't end when the clock struck ten; she, without the smallest experience of 'corporate entertaining', felt she could be positive about that. But, in any case, she suddenly felt she could be equally positive that if Thomson Wakefield had decided to return to the hotel and, on his way out, had spotted the company Jaguar, then she wouldn't at all have put it past him to have come back in and ordered her to drive him back to the hotel. And she, eager as she was to keep this job, would have had to comply.

By the time Yancie was parking at the hotel she had drummed up a fine head of hate against the brute. She was, though, by then, fully confident that he had moved on to continue his evening's entertainment elsewhere. Of a certainty, since she was going straight up to her bed, she ran not the smallest risk of seeing him again that night. The next time she saw him would be tomorrow morning—or so she thought.

It was a cold night and once she had locked up the Jaguar Yancie didn't hang about but hotfooted it into the hotel. Hurrying in, passing a lounge area on her way to Reception, she saw Thomson Wakefield, and stopped dead in her tracks. Their eyes locked full-on. He didn't smile—when did he ever?

Tearing her glance away, and without acknowledging him either, Yancie went swiftly on and out of his sight. She all at once felt all shivery and shaky inside, and she just knew that it had nothing to do with the cold weather.

It had been a shock to come in and see him sitting there nursing a Scotch. What rotten luck; another five minutes and he might have gone to bed. Yancie asked for her key, and was all of a sudden indecisive again, her normal confidence fractured. Should she walk back and say something? What? Goodnight? What if he didn't answer? She'd feel a proper idiot.

To the devil with him. Key in hand, she turned from the reception desk—and discovered that her shocks for the day weren't over. There, endorsing her thought that a few minutes more and her employer would have finished his Scotch and made tracks for his bed, stood Thomson Wakefield, waiting for her.

It was a shock too that, instead of going straight over to the lifts, he was standing near, while she claimed her key, ready to walk over to the lifts with her.

'Good evening?' she enquired as they reached the lifts and he pressed the call button.

Thomson Wakefield didn't answer but looked at her,

his glance taking in her black-lace-covered arms and up-per chest, her lace dress with its modesty lining. 'You're not afraid of catching your death?' he enquired evenly in return, his glance going up from the fine column of her throat to her piled-on-top-of-her-head ash-blonde hair. And suddenly, as his glance fell again to her elegant dress, Yancie just knew that *he knew* that she would never have been able to afford such an expensive item on what Addison Kirk were paying her.

'Er...' She felt left-footed again. 'Um, I forgot to bring a coat,' she mumbled—and was suddenly cross. Hang it all, she sounded more like a fourteen-year-old than the confident twenty-two-year-old she, up until then, had considered herself to be.

'Your uniform jacket didn't quite go?'

Was she being reprimanded? Or—she didn't believe it—was he teasing her? Yancie looked up into his grey eyes—there was something there, but she couldn't be sure. But his reference to her uniform reminded her, if reminding she needed, that she was there only because of her job—the job she very much wanted to keep.

'I haven't been drinking!' she exclaimed hurriedly, apropos of absolutely nothing.

'Did I suggest you had?' he answered mildly, and the lift came and Yancie was glad to step inside.

She watched as, plainly knowing which floor she was on, he pressed the two buttons, and the lift started to ascend. 'You did insist that I had some dinner,' she thought to excuse that she'd been out to dine using the company car.

'So I did,' he agreed, but, his tone cooling slightly, he added, 'It didn't take you long to pick somebody up.'

Pick somebody up! Of all the nerve! All too obvi-ously, this was his way of referring to her escort of the

evening! Yancie, who was trying her very best to behave, felt the restraint she had put herself under all day
getting away from her. Confound it, she *had* been good
all day and on her best behaviour—well, mostly—and,
while she tried hard to let his remark go, she couldn't.
The words just would not stay down.

'I thought he looked a bit of all right,' she replied—
and dared to look at him. And just had to go on looking
at him when, definitely—yes, most definitely—she saw
his lips twitch.

'So how long have you known him?' he asked.

'We were at nursery school together,' she owned. 'I
rang him.' And suddenly she found she was laughing.
She heard Thomson laugh too, stared at him, mesmeri-
sed, saw the way his mouth picked up at the corners,
saw his white even teeth—and was never more glad
when the lift stopped at her floor and the door opened.
'Goodnight,' she said quickly—and went swiftly along
to her room.

Lifts never used to affect her like that, but really—
and it had absolutely nothing to do with the fact that,
coincidentally, she had seen Thomson Wakefield's smile
for the first time, heard him laugh for the first time—she
felt all sort of breathless and fluttery inside.

CHAPTER FOUR

AS IF to make amends for the cold, damp day yesterday had been, Sunday dawned bright and sunny. Yancie was up early and went to shower and dress.

She had no idea what time they were leaving and realised she should have asked Thomson last... Thomson? When had she started to think of him as Thomson? Feeling slightly staggered that her employer's first name rolled around so effortlessly in her thoughts, Yancie knew she had better watch her tongue. The chief of the whole shoot was just going to love it, wasn't he, if his mere driver went up to him with a 'Where are we going to today, Thomson?' type of comment.

Yancie couldn't help but smile as she visualised the affronted expression on his face. But, no time for dawdling. If he wanted to be off straight away, she stood a very real chance of missing her breakfast.

She decided she felt comfortable with her hair up, so pinned it that way. But she left her name tag off, then went down for something to eat. She entered the hotel's dining room and at once saw Thomson, and realised she should have known that he hadn't got where he was by sleeping until midday.

She manufactured up a smile and went over to the table. He stood up and politely waited until she was seated before resuming his seat, but looked at her expectantly when, something very belatedly occurring to her, she exclaimed, 'Oh!'

'Oh?' he queried, and she wanted the ground to open up and swallow her.

'I'll move!' she said abruptly, reaching for her shoulder bag which she'd draped over her chair.

'You're not comfortable here?' he enquired smoothly.

'I've just realised I should be sitting somewhere else,' she said, getting up.

'You should?'

'Do your drivers usually sit with you on these sort of trips?' she asked hurriedly. 'Shouldn't I be sitting in some lowly corner?'

A muscle moved at the side of his mouth, as if she had amused him. But he didn't smile but, still in that same even tone, advised, 'Sit down, Miss Dawkins; I just don't see you ever sitting in some lowly corner.'

She wasn't sure what she was supposed to make of that, but hesitated to sit down again. 'This is embarrassing,' she mumbled.

'Not half as embarrassing as it would be for me if you took yourself off and sat yourself elsewhere,' he assured her.

Yancie sat down. More, she began to realise—as she ate her way through cereal, bacon and egg, followed by toast and marmalade—because finding so unexpectedly that Thomson Wakefield, her taciturn employer, had a great deal of charm.

What else could it be but charm that had made him say he'd be embarrassed if she didn't breakfast at the same table? It wouldn't bother him a scrap if she moved to another table and left him sitting there. From what she knew of him, she'd have said he wouldn't give a hoot where she ate—or whatever table she left his to go and eat at. She could go and perch on the roof for all he cared.

They did not hang about once breakfast was over. But, on the road to London once more, Yancie started to discount entirely that she had for a moment thought Thomson Wakefield had an ounce of charm. He'd got his head stuck in some paperwork—plainly only needing a driver so he didn't waste precious working time by having to drive himself—and had barely moved himself to do more than grunt at her since then.

She glanced at him in the rear-view mirror—his eyes seemed to be focused somewhere at the back of her head. He flicked his eyes upwards—and gave her a sour look. Yancie studied the road up in front, and took pains not to look at her passenger again. Until, that was, about an hour later when the car phone rang.

Her eyes shot in panic to the mirror, and met his full-on. And, of course, he knew what her panic was about. Because, even as he was reaching for the instrument, he was enquiring, 'Are you in if it's your mother?' Sarcastic swine!

Fortunately, he then gave his attention over to the telephone call, which was for him, and she was spared having to make any reply. All too clearly Thomson thought she was the one who had given her mother this telephone number—Yancie wasn't likely to tell him that she hadn't. He must never know that it had been Greville and that Greville Alford was her half-cousin. From there Thomson would quickly, and rightly, conclude it was only because of Greville that she had been taken on by Addison Kirk.

Yancie dropped her passenger off just after two. She would have been a little earlier but, as he had on the outward journey, Thomson had insisted she have a coffee break after a couple of hours of driving.

Yancie supposed she could have driven the Jaguar

straight to the garage once she had said goodbye to her employer—no 'Thank you very much, your driving is excellent', she noticed. On the other hand he hadn't told her—as she was sure he would if it were so—that her driving was lousy and that he'd be reporting it to her head of section. So, she must be thankful for small blessings.

Knowing her mother would be ringing round to trace her if she didn't turn up in answer to yesterday's summons, Yancie decided to drive over to see her mother first.

'You've taken your time!' was her greeting when she got there.

'I'm sorry, I...'

'Come and meet Henry; we've just finished lunch. And what's this I hear about you moving out?'

Oh, heck. 'You know about...'

'I tried to phone you this morning. I smelt something fishy when Ralph told me to try Delia's. He eventually told me you'd moved out, but wouldn't say where to. Delia was out when I rang her and I'd mislaid your car phone number—and I couldn't get Greville.' Thank goodness for that! 'So, what happened to make you leave home? I told Ralph he should be ashamed...'

'It wasn't Ralph's fault!' Yancie cut in quickly. 'Um—the house just wasn't big enough for both Estelle and me, so...'

'She always was a stroppy madam. You should have... Ah, here's Henry!'

Her mother was all smiles suddenly, and although Henry Ottaway, a portly little man, was pleasant enough he didn't have Ralph Proctor's gentle manner. What he did have, however, was a Rolls outside, and, knowing her mother's propensity for spending, Yancie guessed her mother had run through Ralph's handsome settlement, and was now out to replenish her stocks. Yancie felt saddened that she should think that way—but years of knowing her mother had only endorsed that the only person Ursula Proctor would ever love was Ursula Proctor.

Yancie stayed and had tea with them then both her mother and her soon-to-be new stepfather came out to the car with her, her mother inspecting the registration plate, murmuring under her breath, 'Ralph Proctor might have bought you a new one!'

The car was less than a year old! Yancie drove back to the home she shared with her cousins, her mother never ceasing to amaze her. Yancie had considered taking the Jaguar back to the firm's garage, but since Astra had a perfectly good spare garage going begging, and since Yancie would be one of the first in at Addison Kirk tomorrow, it hardly seemed worthwhile. Besides which, by taking the car home she wouldn't have to mess about with public transport.

Yancie had only just finished telling Fennia and Astra about her dinner with dear Charlie Merrett, when her half-cousin Greville, full of apologies, rang to speak to her.

'Don't worry, Greville.' She smiled down the phone to him. 'I'm sure you couldn't have done anything else.'

'You know your mother's tactics resemble water wearing away stone. I did hold out as long as I could. Did she reach you?'

'Yes—but it wasn't a problem,' Yancie quickly tried to assure him.

'That's good. I was hoping you'd either not be in the car when she rang, or be parked up somewhere. It was the tears that did it.'

'Tears?'

'I thought Aunt Ursula was about to break down in tears when she said how she'd tried everywhere.'

Poor Greville. He couldn't bear to see, or in this case hear, a woman in tears. 'Apparently you had a terrific party,' Yancie swiftly changed the subject.

During the week that followed, Yancie was out and about driving many times. She chauffeured Mr Clements a couple of times, and other directors. And once her half-cousin Greville. But never did she drive Thomson Wakefield. She knew from other drivers that he'd been out and about, though.

It was every bit as if, having satisfied himself that she was a decent driver, Thomson had no further use for her services. And that slightly upset Yancie. She would go into work each day feeling quite excited about what the day might bring—and go home each evening feeling quite flat. Though she was positive that it had nothing to do with her not seeing Thomson that day.

Yancie spent a lacklustre weekend, and was driving the Jaguar after dropping her passenger on a local call the following Monday when the car phone rang. She pulled into the side of the road to answer it, and heard her mother's voice. Oh, crumbs; so much for her wishing this number would stay mislaid!

'Since you're already out and about, do you think you could come and pick me up?' *No way! I'm working!* But her mother didn't know that! 'Where are you? I'm at home and my car's in for a service.'

Yancie started to frame her refusal, but then realised she could probably get to her mother's and drop her off where she wanted to go without a soul being any the wiser.

'I can pick you up,' she agreed. 'Can you make your own way back?'

'I'm meeting your aunt Portia for lunch—she can drive me home.'

Yancie put down the phone and raced over to her mother's home—only just remembering as her mother came out of the house that she was wearing a badge that proclaimed 'Yancie Dawkins, Transport Department, The Addison Kirk Group'. Swiftly Yancie unfastened her tag and stowed it away. But, while luck might have been with her on that occasion, it deserted her totally not long afterwards.

They were in the centre of London in the middle of slow-moving traffic with her mother in the front passenger seat and Yancie listening to her talking at length while at the same time watching the car in front. When suddenly—and why she looked over to the pavement at that particular moment she never afterwards knew—but just as all the traffic halted, look across she did, just as a tall, dark-haired business-suited man came out from a building and, his glance searching, quite obviously ready to hail a taxi, he saw instead the Jaguar he'd been a rear-seat passenger in not two weeks ago. Oh, no! Of all the foul luck! Yancie wanted to look away, to pretend she hadn't seen him. Indeed, had the traffic been free-flowing, she might well have put her foot down and shot off.

But no, Thomson Wakefield was looking straight at her—his glance taking in her flawlessly and expensively dressed passenger. He started to come over—and a riot of emotions played havoc in Yancie.

Without so much as a by-your-leave—and why would he?—Thomson opened the rear passenger door and got in. Her mother, never at a loss for words, was the first to speak. 'Do you very much mind?' she demanded in cultured superior tones.

Yancie, her face scarlet with mortification, quickly found her voice. 'Mother, let me introduce Thomson Wakefield. Thomson…' Oh, grief! Too late now. Yancie ploughed on. 'My mother, Mrs Ursula Proctor.'

Yancie fully expected that at any moment now Thomson would pass some remark to the effect that he was commandeering the Jaguar and its driver and that since Mrs Proctor was not on the company's payroll would she mind vacating. But, much to Yancie's relief, not to mention surprise, she heard him do no more than exchange a few pleasantries with her mother.

'I thought I knew all of your friends, Yancie,' her mother ploughed deeper into her daughter's furrow of acute and deep embarrassment. And shrewdly, she commented, 'Though your voice is familiar. Was it you who answered the phone when I rang Yancie on her car phone the other Saturday?'

'I believe it was,' he answered smoothly.

'You must be a frequent passenger in my daughter's car,' Ursula Proctor was just observing, when, to Yancie's undying gratitude, the traffic started to move again.

Her mother's lunch venue wasn't too far distant. Perhaps Yancie could manage to drop her off before any more damage was done. Though how she was going to square it with Thomson Wakefield now her mother had made it clear that she thought the Jaguar belonged to her daughter, Yancie had no idea.

'Yancie is very generous with her lifts,' Thomson informed her mother evenly.

'Well, at least she's learned her lessons and has stopped loaning her car out to all and sundry,' Ursula

Proctor carried on, thinking to add, 'As you probably know, one of her friends wrote off her old car.'

'I didn't know that,' Thomson murmured, and Yancie, this simple lift taking on nightmare proportions, was glad that for once her mother didn't seem to have anything to come back with.

Yancie's respite, however, was short-lived because, as though only breaking to recharge her batteries, her mother was taking a look at her in relation to her own flawless appearance and the impeccable tailoring of the man they were giving a lift to, and as if ashamed, to Yancie's horror, she began holding forth. 'Honestly, Yancie, you used to have more dress sense. You're always wearing that same drab suit! You were wearing it when you came to meet Henry the Sunday before last!' *Thank you, Mother!* It wouldn't take a genius, and Thomson Wakefield was no fool, to work out that after she'd dropped him off the other Sunday she, and the firm's vehicle, had done a bit of private motoring. But it was not over with yet—in fact, it got worse. 'Living with Delia Alford is doing you no good at all!' her mother stated. *Stop! Mother, please stop!* But it was already too late. Their unexpected, uninvited guest, who was most able to put two and two together, was taking an interest.

'Delia Alford?' he queried pleasantly, more interested in discussing people than in drab uniforms, apparently.

'You've met Yancie's aunt Delia?' Ursula Proctor enquired a touch sharply, as if it was her right to be introduced to all her daughter's friends first.

No! No, he hasn't met her! Nor is he likely to. And, thank goodness, this is where you get out. Yancie pulled over to let her out, but before she could push the passenger door open and wish her mother a hasty goodbye

Thomson Wakefield was saying smoothly, 'I believe I may have met her—son.'

Yancie knew it was all over before her mother responded, 'Greville...'

'I'll have to go,' Yancie butted in quickly. 'I'm illegally parked.' But why was she bothering? Thomson didn't need to hear anything more. He'd heard all he needed to hear. To prove it he left the rear of the car and went to open the front passenger door.

'Thank you,' her mother accepted elegantly, and with no idea of the problems she had just caused her daughter she wished them goodbye and went on her way.

What Yancie did not need was for Thomson Wakefield to take the seat her mother had just vacated. 'I wouldn't want your mother to think we're not the best of friends,' he murmured blandly—and Yancie knew, as she pulled away from the kerb, that she was in for it.

But she needed this job—the best she could do was to try and bluff it out. 'Er—do I gather I'm—um—likely to be suspended again?' she went into battle, inviting a discussion on the subject.

'You don't think I should dismiss you?'

Well, as a matter of fact, no, I don't. 'What have I done?' she asked innocently. 'Well, apart from borrowing the firm's motor to visit my mother the other Sunday. And I'm sure you'll see that, since I had been working—and was quite pleased to,' she inserted hastily, 'that...'

Thomson spared her further complicated self-exonerating explanations by cutting in. 'You forgot to mention on your application form—in the space that asks "Do any members of your family work for the company?"—that you're related to one of the directors.'

He had her there. Attack. 'I didn't know you took such a fine interest in your drivers' job applications.'

'With you, Yancie Dawkins, I've discovered it's as well not to take everything on face value.' What did he mean by that? 'Was everything on your application form a lie?'

She wished she could remember! He'd obviously seen her application form more recently than her. 'Er—the address I gave is the right one.'

'Your aunt's address?'

Oh, hang it! 'I'm not living with my aunt, I'm living with my cousins—er, Fennia and Astra. Greville's my half-cousin. He lives...' she broke off; she was rambling.

'I know where Greville Alford lives,' Thomson spared her coolly. But, shaming her, he went on, 'Your mother believes you're living with your aunt.'

'I didn't tell her I was,' she defended, 'I just didn't tell her I wasn't living with Ralph any more.'

A pause followed. A cold, icy kind of pause. 'So that was a lie too, when you said you knew the theory of the facts of life, intimating you hadn't any experience...'

'It wasn't a lie!' she denied hotly—oh, grief, she wasn't doing herself any favours here getting cross. This was no way to go about keeping her job. But she followed his drift, and said more calmly, 'Ralph is my stepfather.'

A few moments of silence ensued, but it didn't last for long before Thomson was questioning—though making it sound more like a statement—'You lived with him until recently?' He didn't wait for her to answer. 'You left your stepfather's home around the time one of your friends wrote off your car.'

'No wonder you're the top man!' Yancie said sniffily.

'Your stepfather was angry and threw you out,' he went on as if she hadn't spoken.

'He did no such thing!' she denied. 'Ralph wanted me to stay. He wants me to go back.'

'But you're refusing to go?'

'It's a pride thing.'

'Which is why you need this job.'

Now we're truly down to the nitty-gritty! It went without saying that Thomson was now fully aware that she had only got this job because she was related to Greville. 'Driving's about the only work I'm qualified for,' she confessed.

'What about housekeeping?' he enquired silkily.

Sneaky devil! She'd put on her job application that her previous job was as a housekeeper—she remembered that. 'It was the truth!' she stated. 'That is, I kept house for Ralph. It's a big house, too,' she added for a little extra importance. Well, she was in trouble here, and knew it.

'I don't doubt it,' Thomson Wakefield rejoined. 'Your mother doesn't know you have a job, does she?'

'I think I can safely say my mother would throw a fit at the very idea of a daughter of hers working for a living,' Yancie replied, after so much deception glad suddenly to be honest. But, her heartbeat quickening all at once, she took her eyes off the road in front for a moment and turned to stare at him. 'Are you saying I still have a job?'

Thomson Wakefield stared back at her, his expression giving nothing away. Then, music in her ears, 'If you think you can bear the uniform,' he replied.

And as her heart rejoiced Yancie looked swiftly away. For a moment there, she felt so overjoyed she could have kissed him—and that would never do. Instead, she suddenly became aware of her surroundings—hadn't they been past that shop there twice before? 'Where are we

going?' she asked hurriedly, and, glancing at him, was
sure she saw his lips briefly twitch before he abruptly
told her to take him back to his office. She was late, of
course, picking up her earlier passenger.

So as not to involve Greville in any prevarications on
her behalf, she contacted him as soon as she could to
say that Thomson Wakefield now knew that they were
half-cousins.

'Was he all right about it?' Greville asked.

Given that he'd all but pulled her back teeth in ex-
tracting from her all that there was to know! 'He was
very kind,' Yancie assured her cousin.

She supposed, when she thought about it, that
Thomson had been kind. It was for certain he'd soon
recognised that her mother didn't know she was working—and he could so easily have given her away, but
hadn't. He could equally have tipped both of them out
of the firm's vehicle, and driven off in it, but hadn't.
Yes, he had a very kind streak in him.

Yancie drove him later that week. But forget kind. He
was back to being the grouch she had first known.
Treating the vehicle as an extension of his office, working away there, with barely a glance at her.

Yancie went home with Thomson on her mind a lot.
And felt all fluttery in her chest the next day when she
happened to be in Kevin Veasey's office when Veronica
Taylor rang down for a car for Thomson.

'Shall I?' Yancie offered, available.

'He wants Frank to do this run,' Kevin smiled.

'Fine,' she smiled back—and felt unbelievably hurt.

She did not drive him for several days after that, and
was sure she didn't give a button. Then, on Wednesday
of the following week, Kevin Veasey told her she would
be driving the Jaguar and Mr Wakefield tomorrow to a

late afternoon meeting in Staffordshire. It was, she fully
owned, ridiculous to feel so cheered. Quite, quite ridiculous.

'Did I hear Kevin say you were going north tomorrow?' Wilf Fisher waylaid her half an hour later.

'You did,' she replied, and felt so extraordinarily
pleased with life just then that when he asked her if she
would mind dropping a parcel of wool oddments off at
his mother's home—Mrs Fisher apparently knitted blankets in her spare time, and was always short of wool—
Yancie was happy to oblige. 'Your mother's home is
quite a bit out of my way,' she qualified, 'but if I'm to
wait any length of time I'd be glad to drop it in for you.'

Wilf was all smiles, Yancie was all smiles; she really
did like her job, she decided. To be out and about. Some
people must like office work but she was glad she didn't
have to do it.

That some people thrived on office work was borne
out the next day when Yancie collected her passenger.
A grunt for a greeting was all she got. And, once in-
stalled in the back of the Jaguar, Thomson Wakefield
undid his briefcase, buried his nose in his paperwork,
and Yancie didn't hear another grunt from him until she
pulled up outside one of their subsidiary companies.

'I'll be finished here at six. Have a rest and something
to eat,' he ordered. *Yes, sir, anything you say, sir.* She
had something better to do! Their eyes met, and Yancie
could only suppose he must have picked up a gleam of
defiance in her eyes, because he questioned bossily,
'Yes?'

Yancie had no idea why his manner should rattle her
so, but, 'Yes,' she agreed—bubbles to that—striving for
a meek note.

What was it about him? she wondered as she headed

out of Staffordshire and into Derbyshire. He had managed to upset her from day one. She wouldn't have got so riled, had any other board member suggested she take a rest and have something to eat. But then, he hadn't suggested, but told. Perhaps she wasn't any good at taking orders. She really must try and get this being employed sorted out.

Wilf Fisher's mother was expecting her, and was very pleased to see her. 'You'll stay for a cup of tea and a piece of cake?' she asked as Yancie handed over the large, bulging plastic sack. To please Mrs Fisher, whom, it appeared, had made the cake especially for her, Yancie said she'd love a cup of tea and a piece of cake, and chatted to her for about half an hour

She was on the point of leaving, however, and was in fact making her goodbyes, when Mrs Fisher suddenly asked if she was going anywhere close to the nearby supermarket.

'I'm sure I must be,' Yancie obliged.

She shouldn't, Yancie knew as she sped down the motorway to Staffordshire, have wandered around the supermarket with Mrs Fisher. But, for goodness' sake, surely she wasn't expected to leave the old dear to carry all that shopping back on her own!

The only trouble now, of course, was that there was no way that she was going to be able to pick up sir at six. He'd have her hide, she knew it. He'd be kept waiting—and she'd like to bet that no one *ever* kept him waiting.

It was ten past six now, and there were miles to go yet. She glanced at the petrol gauge, and found fresh cause to worry. Oh, grief, she was driving again on empty! She normally spent her waiting time filling up and checking her vehicle was ready for the return journey. Only she hadn't this time—and she dared not stop now. She remembered the last time a petrol gauge had registered empty, and how that time she'd come close to disaster. She'd been visiting Mrs Fisher that time too. Perhaps the Fisher family were a jinx on her.

She made a vow there and then to let Wilf Fisher deliver his own parcels in future. Though in fairness it wasn't anybody's fault but her own. She was late because she'd stayed for tea and cake—so all right, Thomson Wakefield had ordered her to take refreshment—he just hadn't expected she'd trip into the next county to carry out his instructions, that was all.

Thomson had been around the last time she'd been rushing back from Derbyshire—he'd been angry then; he'd be furious now. Oh, help, half past six—he'd skin her!

It was ten to seven when Yancie pulled up to collect her employer. She could see at once that he was not a happy man. She opted to stay in the driver's seat—the sooner she got started, the sooner she'd get him back to London.

Though first, as if to deliberately keep her waiting this time, Thomson Wakefield took a slow, methodical walk all around the car, every bit as though checking to see how many dents she had put in it. Sauce! Anyone would think she went around having accidents—there wasn't so much as a scratch on the Jaguar.

Eventually he opened a rear door and got in. Yancie saw it as her cue to prostrate herself at his feet. Fat chance! But, 'I'm sorry,' she began—she owed him that much. Only he didn't want to hear the rest of it.

'Save it!' he snarled.

Yancie was happy to. She had just discovered she had

more of an aversion to lying to him than she'd realised.
Although, in reality, she hadn't any idea what she could
have added to her apology that wouldn't implicate Wilf
Fisher. But in any event Wilf hadn't exactly held a gun
to her head. She could have, and should have—of
course—told him to post his mother the wool parcel,
though it had been more of a sackful than some small,
neat parcel.

Suddenly Yancie became aware that she must have
missed a turn somewhere. Where had the town gone?
By now she should be in a lit-up area heading towards
the motorway. Instead she was in a dark, tree-lined area
with no sign of a motorway. In fact, the road she was
travelling on seemed to be getting narrower and narrower. And where was all the traffic? There was none.
She was in the middle of nowhere with not so much as
a streetlamp about, leave alone another vehicle. Oh,
grief!

'You *do* know where you're going?' enquired a nasty,
disgruntled voice from the back.

And Yancie found she could still conjure up the occasional lie—when desperate. 'I know a short cut,' she
answered, hoping he would think she was taking the
short cut. Icy silence was her answer.

Shame about him. He who liked to work the whole
of the time. It was much too dark to see to read paperwork, much less make a few pencilled notes. Though it
wouldn't surprise her if any minute now he didn't get
out his tape machine and start dictating letters for
Veronica Taylor to type back in the morning.

Then it happened. The engine cut out. Oh, no! How
could she have forgotten? The Jaguar slowed to a stop.
The silence behind her was deafening. 'I...' she found
her voice, slightly strangulated though it sounded '...be-

cause of my rush—er—my fault,' she added hurriedly, 'my fault entirely. I—um—didn't fill up with petrol.'

Silence again; she imagined her disgruntled employer was counting up to ten. She was not flavour of the month, she knew that much anyway when, his voice holding several degrees of frost, he ordered, 'Then perhaps you wouldn't mind filing up with petrol now.'

Yancie was getting seriously fed up with him. 'Where from?' she asked, a touch snappily, she had to own.

'You tell me—I thought you knew this "short cut".'

Swine, pig, toad! He knew full well she had been lying. 'There's a petrol can in the boot,' she hinted. Bubbles to it, if anybody was going for petrol, it was going to be him, not her.

'I'll see you when you get back,' he stated charmingly.

'*Me?*'

'It was your lot who wanted equality of the sexes,' he pointed out, quite fairly, she knew—but it didn't endear him to her any. 'On your way.'

Silently calling him all the foul names she could think of, Yancie got out of the car and opened up the boot. Everything neat and tidy—car rug, first-aid kit. Ah, there it was. She took the can for petrol from the boot and, on a spirit of the moment, took the car rug as well.

She closed the boot, and went and opened the rear passenger door and tossed the car rug inside. 'I may be some time,' she said in the manner of Captain Oates— who had gone and had never come back. She thought she heard a sound that might have been a smothered laugh—but she didn't believe it.

She closed the door and looked about—there was *nothing* to see! Which way? Well, she wasn't going back the way they had come. If there had been a petrol station in the last five miles she'd have noticed it, remembered it, she felt sure of it.

She liked walking, Yancie told herself as she headed in the direction the car had been facing. So, okay, she was wearing two-and-a-half-inch heels and the road was getting more rutty than tarmacked by the minute. Where the dickens was she? Not on any main road, that was for sure. Oh, help, she'd nearly fallen over then.

Yancie concentrated on walking in a straight line—only the road wasn't straight; she went round a bend, knowing she was out of sight of the car, not that Wakefield could see her in the dark—not that he'd be watching. He'd be too busy dictating something or other into that infernal machine.

What was that? She heard a sound, and then another in the trees to her right, and swallowed down fear. *Don't be a sissy; country dwellers hear those sorts of noises the whole time.*

The sound came again, to her left this time. It was so dark, and she was scared, and as the sound came again she knew she definitely hadn't imagined it. There it was again, behind her this time—she hurried up her pace, her mouth drying.

Footsteps! She could have sworn she heard footsteps behind her. Fear gripped her. Here she was, half petrified, while that smug swine Wakefield was comfortably ensconced under a car rug to keep out the chill. Here was she, ploughing through... Her palms went moist... Those were definitely footfalls she'd heard. Somebody was creeping up behind her.

She hurried up her step. *Keep calm, keep calm.* She heard a twig snap not too far away—and then the sound of rapidly approaching feet! Yancie tossed away the petrol container she was carrying and took off.

She did not get very far. Because suddenly, close by, a voice called, 'Yancie, you idiot, it's me!' and she halted in flight. Halted, turned, took a pace, and cannoned straight into Thomson Wakefield—and hit him.

'You pig!' she yelled, her control shot, feeling a mixture of relief and anger that he could so frighten the daylights out of her. Anger with herself that she could be so weak, so pathetic as to be scared—and to indeed feel every bit the idiot he had called her.

'Shh—it's all right,' Thomson attempted to calm her.

She was not to be calmed. 'How dare you sneak up on me?' she yelled, and punched him again, hitting his shoulder. She might have hit him a third time, but he had taken hold of her arms and anchored them to her sides—about the only way to stop her practising on him for a world-title fight.

'Shh...' he said softly again. 'I didn't mean to scare you. I...'

'Well, you did!' she raged, but owned she was feeling much, much better.

'I'm so, so sorry,' he apologised handsomely, and, now that she had stopped hitting him, had one arm around her. Instinctively Yancie leant her head against his chest, feeling better still and comforted, when, as if to hold her there, Thomson placed a hand to the back of her head. And Yancie felt all at once strangely at peace—as if this was where she should be.

But somewhere in her mind she knew that she should break away before Thomson pushed her away. Yet she didn't seem able to move, and he didn't seem in any hurry to let her go.

'You're very kind,' she said against his chest.

'You really *were* scared, weren't you?' he teased.

'You mean to say nobody ever accused you of being

kind before,' she actually heard herself laugh—and once more began to feel back in charge, and the Yancie Dawkins she had always known herself to be. She took a step back, and he let go of her. 'I threw the petrol can away,' she said, somehow knowing that she would never forget those wonderful soothing moments when Thomson Wakefield had held her against him to comfort her. 'We'll never find it; it's much too dark.'

'Suddenly you're "we",' he answered, telling her if she didn't know it that he had no intention of scrabbling around looking for it.

'So,' she said, 'since you're the brains of this outfit, what do you suggest I do?'

'Go to the farm, and see if they can help out.'

'What farm?'

'Didn't you see the lights?'

'You're taller than me.'

'I'll come with you,' he said. She wasn't arguing— she'd had enough of wandering around pitch-black, deserted country roads on her own.

It was quite a way to the farm and she instinctively took hold of Thomson's arm when they left the road, crossed a field and trod ankle-deep in mud. She didn't quite fancy going splat on her face. He didn't seem to object—he didn't shrug her hand off anyhow. In fact, he really was as kind as she'd said, talking to her quietly as they went, seeming more considerate of the fright he'd given her than bothered that his day's work was ending up with him up to his trousers in quagmire.

Yancie was growing to like him more and more as they trudged on to the ever nearing lights shining from the farmhouse. By the time they were knocking on the farmhouse door, she had decided that she was definitely never, ever, going to lie to him again.

'I'm sorry to trouble you...' Thomson began when someone came to the door, and Yancie's heart was warmed when the farmer not only supplied them with some petrol, but insisted on driving them back to their car.

Yancie gave her own thanks to the farmer and left Thomson talking to him as they emptied the fuel into the petrol tank.

She was in the driving seat when the farmer drove off. She started the engine and it purred into life. Then, while she waited for Thomson to get into the back seat of the car, to her surprise, he came and opened the driver's door.

'I'm driving,' he said.

'No, you're not!' she argued—she was the driver. 'And it's cold with the door open.'

The interior light stayed on. Thomson studied her. 'I could pull rank, or I could physically move you.'

Yancie considered her options. 'You're saying you're fed up and you want to go home—and you don't want me to take you on any more short cuts?'

He just looked at her. In any other circumstances she had an idea he might have laughed. But suddenly she was contrite. He'd had a long day, she'd had a long day—and they were both tired. Without saying another word she got out and went round to the other side, opening the front passenger door, absently tossing her shoulder bag from the front passenger seat to the rear.

They were driving along before it suddenly occurred to her to ask, 'Was I supposed to sit in the back?' Thomson didn't answer, but half turned, a trace of amusement on his mouth before he gave his attention back to the road.

Shortly afterwards they stopped to fill up with petrol and Yancie stayed with the front seat. She felt right there. And if Thomson didn't want her sitting next to him, then she full well knew he wouldn't mince words to tell her so.

'Where did you get to this afternoon?' he asked conversationally when they were on their way again.

'Where?' she questioned in return, playing for time, her decision to always tell him the truth soon under attack.

'There were an additional sixty miles on the milometer.'

'Trust you to take a note,' Yancie accused stiffly, knowing she still hadn't got the hang of this being employed lark, though having an idea she shouldn't be answering back. But—really!

'I didn't intentionally,' Thomson answered, quite civilly, she felt, considering she was all snappy and snarly.

'You have a brain that automatically registers numbers?'

'Quite often without me being aware of it,' he agreed. 'So, left with time on your hands, you decided to go and take tea with one of your friends from nursery school who happens to live barely thirty miles distant?'

Yancie by then was forming the opinion that he didn't really want to know, and started to like him afresh that he seemed, by chatting to her in this conversational way, to want to make amends for previously scaring the living daylights out of her.

But, although she hadn't been having tea with one of her old friends, she had been having tea with someone. And, very conscious of his clever brain, Yancie didn't want him prying further when—who knew?—she might inadvertently let the name 'Fisher' slip—and from there

she might get Wilf into trouble. So, 'No,' she said
briefly, 'I didn't.'

'Then you must have been visiting your sister.'

She laughed. 'I don't have a sis...' She stopped laughing.

'You don't?' he questioned evenly. 'You mean there's
no little Miranda-Cassandra?'

Oh, help! Yancie took a glance at him. She thought
she might see him looking angry. But no, if anything he
looked amused that she had been so neatly tripped up.
And it was then that she knew that he had known all
along that she didn't have a sister. All the time she'd
been trotting out that tale about her niece leaving her
inseparable toy behind, he had known she had neither
sister nor niece. That she had been lying her head off.

'I confess,' she owned up—what choice did she have?
'I'm an only child. But,' she hurried on, still desperate
to keep her job, 'I will never, ever, lie to you again.'

She held her breath—was it goodbye time? Thomson
glanced at her. 'Promises, promises,' he said. Yancie
breathed again.

Some while later she recognised they were nearing the
smart area where Astra's father's flat was. '*I* should be
driving *you* home,' she said hurriedly.

'You've had a long and—trying—day,' he answered
kindly.

And Yancie was quite taken suddenly by the fact that
this man she was sitting beside had not barked at her
once in the last couple of hours. She was still feeling a
little bemused by his kindness when, Thomson having
read her address once, apparently, and with his photographic memory filed it away, he pulled the car up outside her home.

She vaguely recalled she had a shoulder bag in the

back somewhere, and stretched an arm back, connected
with it, but in pulling it over she accidentally clipped
Thomson on the ear with it.

Oh, my word, he was not amused. But unfortunately,
at the what-the-hell-are-you-going-to-do-next kind of
look he threw at her, Yancie very nearly collapsed.

Oh, help, she could feel a fit of the giggles coming
on. It was his pained expression that triggered it. She
laughed; he didn't. She strove hard for control—it was
a wasted effort. Thomson got out of the car. *Think of
something awful.* She couldn't.

He came round to the passenger door and Yancie got
out of the car, her eyes brimming with merriment. She
coughed down another giggle as she struggled for control.

Oh, my giddy aunt, she would have sworn she hadn't
had a fit of the giggles since she and her cousins had
been at boarding-school. But, as she stood on the pavement with him, so Yancie knew she was fighting a losing
battle with her giggle-muscles.

She was still swallowing down laughter, or trying to,
when Thomson, standing there silently studying her,
found the cure. 'You're stupid!' he gritted exasperatedly.
And when that only seemed to make her explode into
more giggles he did no more than catch hold of her and,
his head starting to come nearer, he kissed her.

There was not a glimmer of laughter about Yancie
when he pulled back to look down at her. Satisfied, as
she just stood there and stared at him, Thomson, without
so much as a goodnight, turned and walked away.

Walked away and left her with a wild mixture of emotions raging in her. He started up the Jaguar and drove
off, but Yancie didn't move. She had known Thomson

had a wonderful mouth, but had never thought to experience it against her own.

Yet, while it had not been a lover's kiss, or even a friend's kiss, it was a kiss that seemed to shatter all she knew. Her heart, her mind seemed to be in uproar. She felt breathless, dizzy—and had the craziest notion that—if she didn't know better—she'd have said she had fallen in love with him!

CHAPTER FIVE

SHE WAS not, not, not in love with Thomson, Yancie told herself repeatedly as the weekend came and went. She was still telling herself the same thing when Thursday rolled around again—a week, a whole week since she had last seen him—and thoughts of the head man at Addison Kirk seemed to be still totally dominating her mind.

She supposed, on balance, seeing what a hash she'd made of it the last time she'd been called upon to chauffeur him—when he had ended up chauffeuring her—that she couldn't blame him for not requesting her to drive him since. And yet—even though she wasn't in love with him—she missed him. Indeed, sometimes she felt so heartsore, she ached just to see him. But she *wasn't* in love with him!

Yancie occasionally worried that she might be growing to be like her mother, or her cousins' mothers, Aunt Portia or Aunt Imogen. But it didn't feel like it. This— this feeling inside of her wasn't a feeling she got for any one-anywhere-likely-looking man. It was just for— Thomson Wakefield.

It upset her, this new and never-experienced-before emotion. Yet, when she, Astra and Fennia had always been able to discuss absolutely everything, including their innermost thoughts, she felt completely unable to discuss this—whatever it was she felt for Thomson— with them. It was too private. Somehow, it was much too private to share with even her two lovely cousins.

Yancie tried hard to think of something else other than
Thomson, yet thoughts of him seemed to consume her.
Ridiculous, she told herself; totally ridiculous. It was for
sure he wasn't wasting a minute's sleep in thinking of
her. If he were, he'd be on that phone to Kevin asking
for her to drive him somewhere. But had he rung for
her? Had he blazes!

'What's the matter, Yancie?' Fennia asked her when
they met up at Astra's flat that night.

'Matter?'

'You've been—different. All this week you've been
quiet. Sort of as if your mind is elsewhere.'

'I'm sorry,' Yancie apologised.

Fennia shrugged her apology aside. 'You're not having problems at work? With your mother?'

'Oh, Fen!' Here was she, moping about, when Fennia
had much more serious problems. 'How are things with
you and your mother?'

'Like she doesn't want to know.'

'What we need is a party,' Yancie decided to be
cheerful.

'True, but Astra's got a whole load of work on this
weekend, and it wouldn't be fair.'

'So Saturday night's out,' Yancie agreed.

'In which case, I'll take myself off on Saturday to see
my mother—who knows? She might give me a less
frosty reception than last time.'

'Would you like me to come with you?'

'I couldn't let you,' Fennia replied—they both knew
that if Portia Cavendish was not ready to make friends
with her daughter, then her cousin Yancie would be in-
cluded in the permafrost.

'We've been through worse.'

Fennia laughed. 'Do you remember...?'

With Astra busy most of Saturday, and with Fennia planning to call on her mother that evening—Fennia's mother refused to speak to her daughter on the telephone—Yancie, for the first time in her life, felt at a loose end.

She had worked on Saturday morning, getting a Mercedes spruced up. Because she was off to the airport very early on Sunday morning, taking Mr Clements to catch a plane, she was being allowed to take the Mercedes home.

Yancie knew full well that she was not allowed to use the car for personal use but she felt out of sorts, without feeling ill. Felt restless, unsettled and needing to be doing something. She could, she knew, go and pay her mother a visit. And Ralph would always welcome her; she knew that.

But, as ever, she turned to her aunt Delia in this time of needing she knew not what. Yancie drove the Mercedes over to her aunt's home.

'Yancie, my dear, how lovely to see you!' Aunt Delia beamed, warming Yancie's heart immediately. 'Come and tell me all you've been up to.'

Two hours later, while making a determined effort that her aunt should not know she was feeling a little flat just then, Yancie was enjoying her aunt's company when Delia Alford said she'd make some more tea. 'I'll make it!' Yancie straight away volunteered, when just then the telephone rang.

'You answer the phone—I'll make it,' her aunt countermanded at once. 'I don't want to speak to Imogen Kirby if it's her.'

'I'll tell her you're tied up with the plumber.' Yancie laughed, guessing the two half-sisters had had words about something or other.

It was not her aunt Imogen, Astra's mother, on the phone, however, but Matthew Grant, a friend of Greville's, asking if by any chance Greville was there. 'That's not Mrs Alford, is it?' it suddenly dawned on him.

'Guess again,' Yancie suggested, having met Matthew on numerous occasions, and liking him very much.

'You've got to be one of Greville's stunning cousins.'

'Which one?'

'I can't say "the pretty one", because you're all ravishing.'

'I wonder why some girl hasn't snapped you up yet, Matthew?' Yancie laughed. 'It's Yancie. How are things with you?'

'Poor on all fronts. Not only has my girlfriend dumped me, but my car had a slight mishap last night, so I'm without wheels—which is why I'm trying to trace Greville. I'm supposed to be going to a party tonight, and if he's going too he might be able to give me a lift—only he's not home.'

'Hang on; I'll ask my aunt if she knows what he's doing.' Yancie put down the phone and slipped into the kitchen. 'Matthew Grant wants to know if Greville's going to some party or other tonight. Any idea?'

'He's taking his poor dear mother to the theatre,' Greville's wonderful mother replied.

Yancie grinned and went back to the phone, recollecting that Greville was something of a theatre buff, but her grin faded—everybody had something to do that night, it seemed. 'Greville's not going to your party,' she relayed to Matthew, and, on a sudden impulse, she offered, 'I'll drive you if you like. But I can't come back for you,' she added as an afterthought. 'If you can make your own way home.' She knew all about parties. They went on until all hours and she didn't fancy getting out of bed to collect him at any time past midnight when she had to be up at four in the morning to drive to Mr Clements' address.

'Would you?' Matthew seemed a little amazed at her offer, but was soon liking the idea. 'Getting a lift home won't be a problem. There's sure to be someone there going my way,' he accepted, and Yancie was just about to ask him what time he wanted picking up when Matthew had a sudden idea. 'You wouldn't like to come to the party too, would you?'

'I haven't been invited.'

'I've just invited you. I'm supposed to be taking someone—and I don't want all and sundry to know I've just been thrown over. Do come with me, Yancie.'

Poor Matthew; beneath his bright tone he sounded as if he was hurting. 'I won't be able to stay long,' she said, weakening; wasn't a party just what she needed?

'You'll come?' he sounded pleased.

'What time shall I call for you?'

As soon as she put the phone down Yancie knew that she didn't want to go to any party. She had thought she did, but even though she didn't know what she *did* want it wasn't a party. 'I'm taking Matthew Grant to a party he's invited me to tonight,' she smiled to her aunt when she went back to the kitchen.

Yancie, dressed in a straight garment of little material, considering its outrageous price, picked Matthew up at eight-thirty as arranged and drove him to the party. They were warmly welcomed by their hosts and were soon in the swing of things.

Yancie had thought she might see someone she knew, as usually happened at that sort of function. But she saw no one she knew and, while owning that her heart wasn't in it, she did her very best for Matthew's sake.

The party was at its height, however, when he leaned forward and, sounding extremely stressed, exclaimed in hushed tones, 'She's here!'

'Your ex?' Yancie whispered back, keeping her eyes steady on him so whoever 'she' was shouldn't know, by the merest look, that they were talking about her. He nodded, pinning a smile she knew he wasn't feeling on his face. 'Do you want me to be all over you, or to disappear and leave you to try and mend fences?' she sought to help in any way she could.

'Why couldn't I have fallen in love with you?' he asked, looking at her seriously.

Because I wouldn't have wanted you to. 'It's a sad life,' she said, and laughed—and he laughed too—and Yancie, almost as if she could feel his ex-girlfriend's eyes boring into her, just had to look up, over by the door.

They were being observed, she saw, lapsing into stunned shock. Not by a female, though, but by a tall, dark-haired man who was a latecomer to the party. Warm colour seared her skin—the last time she had seen him he'd kissed her to stop her giggling!

Hurriedly she switched her glance away from Thomson. Matthew was saying something, but he could have been babbling away in Esperanto for all she was making any sense of what he was saying.

Thomson! Thomson—here! Her heart was fluttering like crazy; she wanted to go home—she wanted to stay. She wanted to rush out to the Mercedes and... Oh, my lord—the Mercedes. She was dead! He'd seen the car in the drive—he must have done. Did he *know* the car? With his photographic memory for numbers? Stop hoping, Yancie; he probably had every car registration number in the Addison Kirk fleet noted.

'…she can think again!'

Yancie came slowly out of her shock to realise that Matthew had just finished telling her something. 'Er—would you mind very much if I took off now?' she asked him, dragging up a smile from somewhere.

'Oh, Yancie, you couldn't hang on for another half-hour, could you? It's only eleven and I wouldn't mind at all if Pippa caught sight of me captivating the best-looking woman here.'

She didn't want to hang on—she wanted to get out of there, and fast. Thomson Wakefield wasn't interested—but he might have come over to say hello. Since they'd been looking straight at each other, he couldn't pretend he hadn't seen her. Not that she wanted him to come and say hello either. She just wanted to get out of there. She wanted to go home.

So, she stayed, 'Go on, then,' she smiled at Matthew Grant. 'Captivate me.'

He laughed, and she hoped Thomson was watching. Watching and taking note how, if he wasn't interested, then—as some other eager male came up to them—there were others who were.

It was a large room, more of a hall than a drawing room, but Yancie was aware of where in the room Thomson was most of the time. Where he wasn't was anywhere near her!

'I have to be up very early in the morning,' she told Matthew when, in her view, having done a magnificent stint and still there three-quarters of an hour later, she just couldn't take any more. 'Will you say goodbye to our hosts for me, and thank them for me? I'd prefer just to slip off.'

'You're sure? I'll come to your car with you.'

'Oh, good heavens, no!' she smiled. 'No need for that. Stay and...' she had an idea he might be sidling up to his ex fairly shortly '...and the best of luck.'

He kissed her cheek, and Yancie, unable to resist looking where she had last surreptitiously looked, felt completely wretched that she was denied her last sight of Thomson—for he wasn't there.

As if making her way to the cloakroom, for all she hadn't brought a coat, Yancie wandered out from the drawing room. She felt unutterably bereft as, impervious to the cold, she walked down the long line of cars, until she came to the Mercedes.

But that was when her heart started to thunder. She had the Mercedes unlocked when, before she could get into the driver's seat and speed away from there, a voice she would know anywhere quite clearly drawled, 'Well, if it isn't Yancie Dawkins! Fancy seeing you here,' and Thomson Wakefield strolled out of the shadows.

What could a girl do? Instinctively, while most peculiarly she wanted to stay and linger a while with Thomson, she also wanted to rocket out of there. Thomson had come round to stand facing her by the time she'd got herself a little more together.

She decided on a charm offensive—well, you never knew. 'It's a fair cop, guv,' she trotted out, smiling. She could see his face—he wasn't smiling. 'How about— I've a widowed mother and six siblings to support?' she pressed on, feeling suddenly desperate not to lose her job, but realising that she was going to have to be exceedingly lucky to keep it.

'You forget, I've met your mother—you couldn't make enough in a year to support her monthly expenses,' he replied.

Yancie stared up into his unsmiling expression. 'You're going to sack me, aren't you?' she questioned, all bravado gone.

'Give me one good reason why I shouldn't,' he invited, fair to the last, she realised.

But she didn't have any good reason. And to go partying in one of the firm's vehicles—a Mercedes, no less—was something that was most definitely against the rules. It was, equally definitely, something that would be frowned upon and was, without doubt, a sackable offence.

'If—if you sack me then the—er—business will suffer,' she brought out of a despairing nowhere.

Thomson continued to stare, unsmiling, at her. 'Intriguing,' he allowed. 'You're suggesting you're doing a deal somewhere which will collapse if you're not on the payroll to finalise it?'

Sarcastic toad! But she still wanted her job. 'Not me, but Douglas Clements might be doing that kind of a deal. I'm picking him up to take him to the airport at five in the morning. He might miss his plane and jeopardise his whole mission if he can't find alternative transport when I don't show up.'

She wished she could read Thomson's eyes, but they were giving nothing away. 'Then you'd better go home to bed, hadn't you?' he remarked at length. 'I imagine you're going to be up very early.'

Her heart picked up speed. 'Have I still got my job?' she asked eagerly. 'Or do you intend I should do just this one job from expediency, then see to it I'm dismissed as soon as I get to work on Monday?'

'You know better than that!' he clipped, curtly—and she rather thought she did.

'I'm sorry,' she apologised at once, and, having just

added insult to the rest of her crimes, she decided it
might be an idea to get out of there before she said
something that might annoy him some more—when he
wouldn't give her another chance.

She had turned about to open the driver's door, when
Thomson put his hand on her arm to stay her, his hand
remaining on her upper arm, an exclamation leaving
him. 'Ye gods, you're like ice!' he added—it didn't feel
that way to her; his touch, his skin against her skin was
burning. 'Where's your coat?' he demanded.

'I didn't bring one!'

He did not comment adversely on that, as she fully
expected, but, ever a man of decisions, in next to no
time he had shrugged out of his jacket, and was wrap-
ping its delicious warmth about her.

She was, she started to realise only then, freezing.
Thomson Wakefield apparently had the power to make
her forget all about the skimpiness of her attire on such
a cold night. Feeling quite dazed, Yancie turned again
to open the driver's door. But found that Thomson was
directing her to the passenger's door.

'I'll drive,' he said, and they were both in the car
heading down the drive before she got her wits back.

'Where are we going?' she asked, which she owned
wasn't the brightest of questions. 'I mean, if you're driving me home, you'll need the car to get back to the party,
and I won't have a car to take Doug…'

'I'm not going back to the party.'

'You're not?' she questioned, but managed to find a
little more brain power from somewhere. 'Oh, Thomson,
I… Oh, heck!' she mumbled, realising she had just
called the head of Addison Kirk by his first name. 'Is
that a sackable offence?' she asked. He laughed, just as
if he couldn't help it; he laughed, and she loved it, as

she loved him. 'I'm sorry,' she went on swiftly, not ready yet to more fully acknowledge this world-shattering thing that had happened to her. 'I didn't want to spoil the evening for you.'

'You haven't,' he assured her, his laughter gone but his tone pleasant.

'You were thinking of leaving the party anyway?' she began to question, and then thought of something else. 'Did you spot me—nonchalantly—on my way out?'

'Too casual to be true,' he commented.

'You really are kind. As I may have mentioned before,' she added. And added too, only hurriedly, 'I'm not trying to butter you up, honestly, but you could have...' Her voice faded; she started to feel a fool. 'So what's happening?' she asked unhappily.

'What's happening,' he took up, 'since we're heading in your general direction, is that I'm going to drive as far as my place, and you're taking this car the rest of the way.'

'I see,' she murmured. 'You're—um—not going back to the party.' Somehow, she seemed more than a little confused, and even though he'd already said he wasn't going back to the party she felt a need to get everything crystal-clear in her head.

'And neither are you,' he stated.

'I'm not?'

'You're not,' he promised her firmly.

Well, that was clear enough. 'Where's your car, by the way—the Aston Martin?'

'Where I parked it,' he replied, which to her mind was no kind of an answer. But it seemed she had recently come through a very sticky patch, and since by the skin of her teeth it seemed she still had her job Yancie decided not to push it.

So, 'Thank you,' she said prettily.

'What for?'

Not to go overboard—for being absolutely wonderful. 'For letting me keep my job.'

'So what's with this pride thing?'

'Pride thing?'

'You said you needed this job,' he reminded her. 'That it was a pride thing.'

'Ah.'

'"Ah", as in?'

'As in you know so much, there's little more to tell.'

Silence reigned for several seconds. Then, 'You're not going to leave it there, are you?' Thomson asked, and, fantastically, sounded in a very good humor.

'We're nearly at your house,' she said, recognising that part of the road.

'So?'

'So my stepfather—and rightly so,' she inserted fairly, 'was a little displeased when I lent my car to a friend and...'

'And said friend concertinaed it.'

Her mother had acquainted him with the fact. 'Exactly,' Yancie agreed.

'You normally get on with the stepfather? Presumably—since your mother's just got engaged—her ex-husband?'

'I get on very well with him,' she agreed. 'In point of fact, Ralph's a dear, and I love him very much, and he had every right to be cross with me.'

'But?'

'But—well, nothing, really.'

'But?' Thomson repeated—a man, she guessed, who seldom repeated a question. She roused herself to answer as requested.

'Well, he was rightly cross, as I said, and I would have taken a telling-off as my due.'

'Only?'

'Only my stepsister, Estelle, surprised me by chipping in and saying she hoped I wouldn't expect her father to buy me another car. I'd honestly no idea she resented me so much! Anyhow, when I said I'd pay for a new car out of my allowance, Estelle reminded me it was an allowance her father paid me, and—and...' her voice faltered.

'And even though you worked unpaid as his house-keeper you knew you could never take another penny from your stepfather,' Thomson finished for her, and Yancie turned in her seat and stared at him.

'How do you know me so well?' she gasped.

The corner of his mouth twitched. 'I don't—I'm learning all the time.'

He made that sound so nice that Yancie was near to crumbling as he slowed the car and steered it up the drive to his house. That, she felt, as he pulled up at his door, had to be the most terrific drive of her life. The trouble was that she didn't want to part from him—yet had absolutely no reason to linger.

Yancie quickly pulled herself together. Good grief, they'd just been talking of pride—had she none where he was concerned? Acting on the moment, as Thomson started to come round to the passenger's door, she quickly got out and pinned a bright smile on her face.

'Thanks for the loan of the jacket!' she said cheer-fully, taking it off and handing it to him—at once feeling in danger of getting frost-bite as the cold night air nipped.

Thomson looked at her—five feet eight, slender and

totally feminine. 'You'll be all right driving on your own at this hour?'

She looked back at him and sorely needed some back-bone—she was in danger of melting. 'You'll have to watch that, Wakefield,' she jibed. 'Your gentlemanly streak is showing!'

He studied her. 'Are you always looking for trouble?' he asked good-humouredly.

'It always seems to find me without me having to look for it especially,' she laughed—and then, as the cold night bit, she shivered—and Thomson took decisive action.

'You can't go home like that. You'd better come in; I'll get you a sweater.'

'I wouldn't dream...' She was talking to herself. He was already unlocking the door to his house, and he still had the car keys. 'You don't have to...' she protested anyway, following him in. 'Once I'm inside the car's heater will...'

'You've next to nothing on.' He closed the door behind her, and was totally intransigent. 'With those bitty shoulder straps you're all bare arms and bare chest.'

'Thanks,' she said sniffily.

And suddenly he seemed to relent. From being several paces away from her he all at once came back to her.

'Give way, Yancie,' he said softly, and at his tone she was melting again. 'I'm not happy about your driving through London, stopping at traffic lights, dressed as you are.'

Because I'm an employee and you don't want the responsibility of someone opening a car door and getting in beside me? Just because I'm an employee? 'I'll lock myself in,' she said.

'Of course you will,' he answered. But instructed, 'Wait there.'

She didn't, of course. Though she didn't go far. She watched him go up the curving staircase and then, her mind on him more than what she was doing, she wandered off to the room she had been in before—his drawing room.

Thomson did not keep her waiting but returned in no time, carrying a blue cashmere sweater which he handed to her. 'I'll take the very best care of it,' she promised solemnly—and again knew the greatest reluctance to leave—heaven alone knew when, if ever, she might see him again. 'Goodnight, then,' she said.

'Put the sweater on,' he said.

'Oh! Right!' she answered, though instead of putting it on—and she just couldn't believe it—she actually heard herself say, 'You realise, of course, that you've done me out of my goodnight kiss?' Had *she* said that? Had she actually said those words? Had she really invited Thomson to kiss her? Was she so starved of love that she had to beg?

She wanted to apologise, to run—oh, heaven help her, Thomson was looking at her as if he couldn't believe his hearing either! Yancie could have wept from the embarrassment of it. But Thomson was coming nearer and there was suddenly a glint in his eyes which she was a little unsure about.

And while she stood there staring, wanting her words back, he calmly took the sweater out of her hands and dropped it on the back of a chair, remarking, 'I find it quite astounding, Yancie Dawkins, that you're still a virgin.'

'I...' she tried, but her voice died in her throat as he came that little bit closer—but she no longer wanted to run because, while giving her all the time in the world to do just that if she so wished, Thomson was reaching for her.

He looked down into her wide blue eyes and, when she had no other comment to make, he gently pulled her closer to him. As his head came down, Yancie closed her eyes, her heart giving a great quivering sigh of gladness when his sensational mouth touched hers.

It wasn't a brief touch of his lips to hers, but was firm as well as gentle, and her legs went weak. Involuntarily, her hands went to his waist, and she held onto him. He was warm and wonderful and he held her to him and, as gently as it had begun, his kiss ended.

Thomson pulled back, and Yancie stared up at him. 'That was s-some goodnight kiss,' she murmured huskily, and knew she should let go of him and get out of there. But she didn't want to go and, since Thomson still had his arms around her, it didn't look as if he wanted her to go either.

In fact, he was still looking warmly down into her upturned face when he enquired softly, 'I don't suppose you'd care for another?'

Yancie smiled dreamily up at him, and if that wasn't enough of an answer she moved her hands from merely holding his waist, and put her arms around him. And, as she had known, Thomson was quicker than most on the uptake. The next she knew was that his mouth was capturing hers, and he was kissing her again, only this time it was a little different.

And since she was fully cooperating, giving him kiss for kiss, his mouth ceased merely giving but sought and took, and Yancie held tightly onto him. She had been kissed before, but there had always been a shut-off point, a so far but no further point. But, as Thomson's kisses

deepened, so that invisible barrier was reached, and as
he took her with him to one of the sofas in the room, so
as new and exciting emotions started to rock her, her
shut-off point was sublimely passed with Yancie being
completely unaware of it.

All she was aware of as Thomson trailed kisses down
her throat and over her shoulders was that this was the
salve she needed to the loneliness of spirit she had en-
dured each day that she had not seen him.

Then somehow she was on the wide sofa with him,
Thomson half lying over her. He raised his head and
looked into her warm, inviting eyes. 'You're so lovely,
Yancie,' he murmured, 'so beautiful,' and again he
kissed her, his long, sensitive fingers caressing her shoulders, brushing aside the fine shoulder straps of her dress,
and Yancie wanted to be beautiful—for him.

But, even while she knew that she was willing to go
wherever he led, suddenly, when gently, sensitively his
hand caressed down to her breast, and she felt his
warmth as he teased the hard pink tip, and she became
aware that his intimate touch was on the inside and not
outside of her dress, some unwanted kind of hesitancy
started to stir in her which she did not want to stir.

To defy it, she held onto him, and, when he raised his
head again, she kissed him. And would deny him nothing when he lowered his head once more and kissed her
naked breast, taking its aroused pink apex into his
mouth, causing her to clutch him from the pure pleasure
of it.

To say no was nowhere in her mind. How could she
say no, when she didn't want to say no? Why should
she say no? She loved him—what else mattered?

But something did matter, and she hated that it did,
be it her inner convictions grown over the years, or the

knowledge that this love she bore for Thomson was so utterly one-sided; she was too emotionally involved to be able to sort out what.

All she knew just then was that, while she wanted to continue to be held by Thomson, while she was aching to continue to make love with him, she couldn't—something was holding her back.

She felt his hand on her thigh. 'Thomson,' she cried, and she guessed he must have picked up that something in her cry that wasn't yes, yes, yes, because his hand stilled, moved from her thigh, and came up to her chin.

'Yancie?' he queried, propping himself up on one elbow and looking down at her.

'Oh, Thomson,' she lamented, 'I know I'm giving you all the—er—f-full-speed-ahead s-signals, but...'

She had no need to go on; she knew that as soon as he began to straighten her shoulder straps—and that was before he took up, 'But you're not sure.'

He didn't add anything, but sat up, moving her to sit up. And, once sitting beside him, while with most of her she wanted to lie down with him again, to feel again the warmth of his embrace, there was that part of her that still said no.

'I'm sorry,' she said, starting to feel absolutely dreadful, particularly as Thomson was taking this halt to the proceedings so extremely well. 'I d-don't suppose this has ever happened to you before.'

He smiled then, and she felt as if her heart would burst with the love she had for him when he gently tapped her on the nose, and dryly commented, 'With you, Yancie, I'm learning it's wise to expect the unexpected.' And, while finding herself in such strange territory she had no clue to what she should do next, he stood up and went and collected the blue sweater from the chair. 'Come

on,' he instructed. 'If you go now you might manage to
get in a couple of hours' sleep before you have to get
up again.'

Yancie left the sofa, and obediently pulled the sweater
down over her head. 'I'm sorry,' she repeated as
Thomson went with her to the front door.

'You're all right to drive?' he questioned.

'Yes, fine,' she answered, and as he unlocked the car
and handed her the key she found that, away from the
sofa, away from the drawing room, the house, the cold
night air had some small sobering effect. She looked up
at him, some tiny portion of her equilibrium restored.
'Goodnight, Mr Wakefield, sir,' she managed lightly,
and as he looked down at her she promptly had her equilibrium shattered when he bent and saluted her mouth
with his own.

Then abruptly he stood back. 'Go home,' he ordered
her sternly—and Yancie went.

CHAPTER SIX

YANCIE recalled Thomson's sternly voiced 'Go home' many times in the days that followed. And the more she thought about it, the more she began to wonder, rather lovingly, it had to be admitted, if his sternness had stemmed from him being more affected by their love-making, by that final kiss, than he was showing; more affected than he wanted her to see?

It was wishful thinking, she decided, when all days merged into one and she didn't so much as get a glimpse of him. If Thomson had been anywhere at all affected—perhaps more than was normal when male biological urges were let off the leash for a little while—then he had a peculiar way of showing it. She knew darn well he was in business, and that from time to time he'd call for a driver. But did he ever call on her to drive him? Did he blazes!

Unhappily, Yancie was discovering the very hard fact that being in love was painful. Being in love left her open to all manner of hurts and imagined slights. She had tried to deny that she had fallen in love with the brute, but that denial hadn't taken long to come and trip her up. She had known for sure how she felt about him on Saturday night. He'd taken off his jacket and wrapped it around her—and she'd known. It was just there, her love for him. And it was no good hoping it would just as swiftly go away again, because it just wouldn't, and no amount of wishing would make it.

She had fallen in love with Thomson, and she could

do nothing to change that fact. Though, having fallen in love, she instinctively knew that he was the only man she wanted to be with. She just knew she would feel tremendously outraged should any other man attempt to kiss her in the way that he had done.

This self-knowledge brought her enormous relief. Because not only had she discovered that she had all the same natural wanting emotions of any other woman in love; Yancie now knew that she no longer had any need to fear she was like her flighty, fickle-hearted mother, or either of her aunts. Yancie realised that she had feared needlessly in those years of guarding against being like her mother. She was nothing like her in that fast and loose respect. Yancie knew then that she was not in the least permissive, nor ever likely to be. While she had truly wanted Thomson, her wanting was all part of her being so totally heart and soul in love with him.

But, while she was truly in love with him, she would not fully give of herself easily, but only when the time was right. And the time hadn't been right last Saturday, she now realised. She started to cringe at her intimation that, because he'd turned up at the party, she'd had to leave early, thereby depriving herself of a goodnight kiss from her escort. Oh, how could she have invited Thomson to do the honours instead?

It was that invitation that had instigated their love-making, and from which had come her recent awareness of her love for him—and her need for the solace of his arms.

Yes, even then she'd felt starved of love—his love. Her love for him had been growing in her all the while. But—and that was the crux of the matter—Thomson did not love her. Making love with him would mean everything to her—but absolutely nothing to him.

But, throughout her present despond, Yancie found that life went on. She had delivered Douglas Clements to the airport on time. Matthew Grant, obviously having obtained her address from Greville, had sent her 'Thank You' flowers, so presumably all was well again with him and his ex. Fennia's mother wasn't any more friendly to her daughter, and Astra was working as hard as ever.

Like somebody else I know, Yancie sighed, wondering how much more of what she saw as being ostracised by Thomson Wakefield she could take. She didn't know what else she could call it but ostracism, she mused unhappily when she went into work on Friday morning. He hadn't asked for her to drive him anywhere—she might just not exist so far as he was concerned.

Pride at that moment came to her aid. Well, bubbles to him. She didn't care. If he asked her to drive him now she jolly well wouldn't. Ralph had phoned only last night practically begging her to go home—Estelle had upset the housekeeper and the housekeeper had walked out. Ralph had said if she was still too upset to accept her allowance then he would pay her to do his housekeeping, but, whether she took over that role or not, he wanted her home. *So there, Mr lordly Thomson Wakefield—I can easily get another job if I want to.*

She looked up from some paperwork she was completing—everybody had to fill in forms, apparently—to see Kevin Veasey heading her way. She pinned a smile on her face. 'How do you feel about a trip to Manchester?' he asked.

'Love to,' she answered; she had intended to do a little household shopping in her lunch hour, but she could as easily do it tomorrow.

'You won't be back till late,' he warned.

'No problem,' she smiled. 'Who's my passenger?'

'Mr Wakefield,' he replied, and while Yancie felt a
roaring in her ears as her heart went into thunderous
overdrive he added, 'If you'll explain to him that Frank's
wife has started to have her baby a month early...'

'Frank was going to drive him?'

'Nothing personal,' Kevin smiled. 'Frank was going
to come in late because this trip means getting back late,
but he's just phoned in. You'd better get off now, if you
wouldn't mind.'

She should have minded. If her pride hadn't chosen
that moment to go into hiding, what she should have
done—knowing full well that all the other drivers were
out on other assignments, and that she was the only one
available—was to tell Kevin Veasey that she was leaving, as of now, to take up another job. But so much for
her proud determination that she wouldn't jolly well
drive Thomson Wakefield again, even if he asked her.
What she did say to Kevin was, 'May I take the Jag?'

It was another miserable, murky day, yet for Yancie,
as she pulled up the Jaguar outside Thomson's house,
the sun was shining. She'd missed him so much, and
hadn't seen him since the very early hours of last Sunday
morning when he'd stood on this same drive with her
and told her to 'Go home'.

Her heart was pounding against her ribs and she felt
nervous suddenly, torn between a desire to stay exactly
where she was in the car until he came out looking for
his driver, and wanting to go and knock on his door the
sooner to see him.

Be professional, she urged, and left the car to go and
report that his driver was here. At his door she raised
the heavy knocker and clouted the striking plate with it.
She swallowed hard as she waited, issuing useless in-

structions to her brain not to make her face go crimson when she saw him again.

The door opened—but it wasn't him. A tall, angular woman of about sixty who looked as if she'd been on a diet of vinegar and lemons—no prizes for guessing whose mother she was—looked her over. And, obviously recognising the brown suit and beige shirt for the uniform that it was, complete with the name badge identifying Yancie as working for the Addison Kirk group, she ordered arrogantly, 'Wait in the car! My son will be with you presently.' And, with that, she closed the door.

Well! Even Thomson had had the manners to invite her in and to go and get a cup of coffee, Yancie fumed, in two minds about getting in the Jaguar and driving it straight back to the transport section again.

She didn't, however—her need to see Thomson overrode that—but some form of protest was needed. She took off her name badge and tossed it into a pyracantha shrub growing against a wall.

Perhaps the old trout improved with knowing, Yancie mused as she waited. She recalled how Thomson seemed a sour individual too when she had first known him. And then she'd heard him laugh, seen him laugh, seen how laughter lightened him, made him...

Yancie snapped out of it. If she went on like this she'd be a drooling wreck by the time he appeared. She picked up the car phone and dialled. Astra was working from home that morning. 'Hello, it's me,' she said when her cousin answered. 'Just ringing to say I'll be late home tonight,' she went on, and Astra, for once giving work a rest for a few minutes, seemed ready for a chat.

Yancie was still on the phone when the door of the house opened, and briefcase in hand, Thomson came out. Hot colour seared her skin, she turned her head so he shouldn't see, and concentrated hard on keeping her voice even as she started to wind up her call.

Thomson was in the car, the door snapped to, before she'd finished. 'I'll see you when I get back,' she said down the phone, her eyes meeting his in the rear-view mirror—he didn't look as if he'd got out of bed on the sunny side, a glare of impatience her reward for dropping everything to come and get him—even if she was paid to do it! 'Manchester beckons,' she said light-heartedly to her cousin—well, she'd be darned if she'd let *him* know how ridiculously out of sorts just one frown from him could make her. 'Bye,' she smiled down the phone to Astra, and, replacing the phone, she kept her smile in place as, 'Good morning,' she greeted her employer.

'Where's Frank?'

And how are you this morning, Yancie? Not suffering nightmares from the time I almost seduced the pants off you, I hope. Calm down, calm down. 'He and his wife have gone into premature labour,' she replied, and set the car in motion.

Thomson ignored her, and undid his briefcase. My stars, to think she'd been overjoyed to get this unexpected assignment today! She drove out onto the main road, flicking a glance into the rear-view mirror. Their eyes met; she loved him, but last Saturday night could never have been—and she hated him.

She flicked another glance at him. 'Keep your eyes on the road!' he rapped.

Pig! 'I didn't know you still lived with your mother,' she observed sweetly, glanced in the mirror again and saw he'd nearly cracked his face there for a second.

But no, he was determined, it seemed, to be as sour as she'd just thought him, and there was not so much as a glimmer of a smile about him when he barked, 'My mother's staying for a few days while the decorators are at her place.'

Yancie opened her mouth to make some sort of a reply, but saw, as his head bent, that he was already regretting having explained anything at all to her, and that he was more interested in the contents of his briefcase than in any further conversation with her. Well, see if she cared; he'd speak before she did!

And so it was in silence that she drove, exchanging the M1 for the M6, and, while the sun in her life started to grow more and more clouded over, the murky, bitterly cold day turned into a foggy, bitterly cold day the further north they went.

Kevin had told her that Mr Wakefield had a meeting at two o'clock—she did her best to get him there on time, but all the odds were against her. For not only was the fog becoming denser and denser by the mile, causing her to drive with extreme caution, but that day seemed to be the day for roadworks being in progress every other half-mile.

Knowing how Thomson's work seemed to be his lifeblood, Yancie started to feel a little desperate that she wouldn't be able to get him to his meeting on time. And yet, in these ghastly conditions, she didn't want to drive any faster.

If he'd been at all affable she might well have apologised. But, although he was no longer concentrating on his papers, and had his eyes on the road, he didn't have anything to say. Which could mean, she supposed, that he fully appreciated anyhow that nobody but an idiot would speed in these conditions.

Yancie got him to his venue at ten to three. She felt exhausted, her eyes tired and gritty from strain. 'I'm go-

ing to be later than planned,' he said as he snapped his
briefcase shut.

'I'll cancel my date,' she replied pleasantly—she who
was never going to lie to him again.

Without another word Thomson left her to go and
chair his meeting. Yancie guessed she wouldn't see him
again much before seven, but she was feeling down
again and went and parked the car and then went and
had something to eat. She calculated as she fed her inner
person that if Thomson's meeting ended around seven,
then he was going to miss his dinner. He could, of
course, have been planning to stop for dinner somewhere
on the way back. But now that she was driving him she
somehow didn't think he'd bother. In normal times
Yancie thought she would probably have got him home
in three hours or so. But if the fog was still around tonight, then who knew what time they'd get back?

She wondered whether to take him a bun or something
else to eat, then scolded herself for being an idiot.
Thomson was a grown man, for goodness' sake. He was
as capable as she of working out the chances of him
ending the day dinnerless. If he felt in the slightest hungry he was more than able to send somebody out for
some nourishment.

That settled tidily in her head, Yancie went and pur-
chased a couple of packages of sandwiches anyway.
Which, because she had her larger-capacity bag with her
today in anticipation of the shopping she'd intended doing during her lunch break, went neatly inside. If he
didn't mention food, then she wouldn't either.

Yancie had a walk around and then later she went and
collected the Jaguar. She listened to the news on the car
radio—the road traffic report was not good. At half past
six she pulled up outside the venue, and prepared to

wait. She had waited only twenty minutes, however, when the doors opened and Thomson and several businessmen came out. There were handshakes all around, then he was coming over to the car.

She'd wasted a 'Good morning' on him earlier—she didn't bother with a 'Good evening', and he was likewise as talkative. The fog had worsened, grown denser instead of clearing. Should she tell him now that the motorway was closed, or save it?

She started up the car and steered into traffic, and still hadn't told him when, a few miles later, 'Pull over,' ordered a voice from the back. They were still in a built-up area, but there was no mistaking that the weather had deteriorated—soon visibility would be down to nil. Yancie drove on until she found a safe stopping place—perhaps he'd forgotten something and they needed to go back for it. But nothing so simple. 'I'll drive,' he stated crisply. The sauce of it!

'No, you won't!' she argued—but she was wasting her breath; he had come round to the driver's door and had it open, and was waiting—not very patiently—for her to get out. She guessed he was tired and didn't want any argument. And normally that wouldn't have bothered her. But love did funny things to you, and she found she had pared her marshalled argument down to a minimal, 'Driving's my job!'

Unthinkingly she went and occupied the front passenger seat—it was getting to be a habit. Well, she wasn't going to ask him to stop so she could get in the back. He wanted to drive; he could put up with where his passenger chose to sit.

'Er...' she began when she saw he was heading for the motorway. She had his attention; he was listening. 'I'm afraid we're going to have to take the scenic route.'

In this fog? You wouldn't see the proverbial hand in front of you! But he was waiting for the rest of it. 'I tuned in to the news earlier—there's been a pile-up on the motorway. The motorway's closed.' A grunt was all the reply she got. Perhaps if she behaved herself he'd allow her to do some of the driving when his over-concentrating eyes got tired and gritty.

However, it didn't come to that. They were out of the built-up area and had been driving at a snail's pace for some while when the dim entrance lights of a hotel appeared out of the gloom. 'It's ridiculous to go on any further!' Thomson announced curtly.

Yancie couldn't have agreed with him more. At the pace they were travelling, if they reached London by midday tomorrow they'd be lucky! Thomson steered the car cautiously up the hotel drive and pulled up. When he got out of the car Yancie got out too and went inside with him. Though they were out of luck when Thomson tried to book them a couple of rooms—everyone else on the road that night had given up driving as being hopeless, apparently, and there wasn't a room to be had.

'There's the Gainsborough Hotel about a mile down the road; they might be able to help you,' the receptionist, working hard because of unexpected influx of guests, tried to be helpful.

'Do you have their number?' Thomson asked, giving the receptionist the benefit of his charm.

'Shall I ring them for you?' she offered, as busy as she was.

A few minutes later, the last two vacant rooms at the Gainsborough Hotel reserved for them, they went out into the dreadful night. 'Would you like me to drive?' Yancie offered; in her view he'd done a fair enough stint already given the filthy weather.

'No,' he grunted.

Get on with it, then, she fumed. He could be charming to everyone but her! Her mutiny soon faded, however; it was really treacherous out here. She knew she was a good driver, but she couldn't fault his driving. And, if she had to be driven by anyone on such an evening, she couldn't think of anybody she would have chosen other than him.

Eventually they made it to the drive of the Gainsborough Hotel, where it seemed the car park area was full to overflowing. 'Go in while I find somewhere to park,' Thomson instructed, pulling up outside the entrance to the hotel.

It was on the tip of her tongue to say a cheery 'Don't get lost' but she thought he wouldn't appreciate it. So, obediently she got out of the car and went into the hotel, and found it was packed with people thronging about. Given that some of the guests couldn't have anticipated not sleeping in their own beds that night, they seemed to have quickly adjusted, to the extent there was even a faint feeling of a party atmosphere about the place. There were two receptionists on duty. One was busy dealing with a guest, and Yancie gave preference to an elderly couple who had just come in and were enquiring about a room for the night. Then the other receptionist was free.

'You've two rooms reserved in the name of Wakefield,' Yancie began, and when the receptionist placed a couple of room keys on top of the reception counter and passed over a couple of registration cards Yancie saw no reason not to begin filling them in.

She had already made a start when she heard the elderly man next to her cry anxiously, 'Oh, dear. No rooms! My wife's only recently had a hip replacement,

and I really don't think I'm up to driving any more tonight!'

I shouldn't think so either. Yancie stopped writing
while she waited for the receptionist to conjure up a
room out of thin air. But no, even though the woman's
tone was most sympathetic, she couldn't, it seemed, perform this particular trick. 'I'm sorry,' the receptionist
apologised, 'every room is taken; we're even allowing
people to sleep in the lounge areas, but I just haven't
got another room.' But, prepared to go to extraordinary
lengths in the circumstances, she added, 'The lounge
area's going to be crowded, but there's a chair in the
office if...'

Yancie couldn't take any more. She pushed one of the
keys across to the man, and also handed him one of the
registration cards. 'I only need one room,' she smiled.
Well, she did, and she was sure Thomson wouldn't mind
when she told him he'd be perching on an office chair
that night. She smiled in acknowledgement of their gratitude and finished completing the one registration card
and, endeavouring to think in advance, certain there
would be the usual toiletries in the room, she asked the
receptionist if there was any chance of being given
toothpaste.

'Nobody's got round to thinking about that yet,' she
smiled, clearly very pleased that the elderly couple
would be able to get a good night's rest. 'I can do better
than just toothpaste,' she said cheerfully, and went away,
to return with a sample tube of toothpaste, and a couple
of toothbrushes.

Yancie thanked her, discovered the kitchen staff were
going flat out, but that there'd be some sort of a meal
for everyone that night—though since the hotel was

bursting at the seams where they were all going to sit might take more organising.

She came away from the desk, to hear another hopeful trying to get a room. With only one key in her hand she moved over to a spot where she could watch for Thomson to come in. And suddenly she began to experience a few anxieties of her own—about having given his room away. She didn't regret it. How could she? She was sure that she would only have to explain about the elderly couple, about the lady's recent operation... Besides, no one would make anybody drive on a night like this—least of all an elderly gentleman.

With her eyes glued to the door, Yancie saw Thomson, briefcase in hand, come in. Whimsically she felt she might have done him a favour. If he intended to work through the night, wouldn't a chair in the office be ideal?

He saw her at once and came through the scrum to where she was standing. And Yancie knew then that it wasn't whimsy, but nerves—he was going to kill her; she knew it for a fact. 'I've filled in the registration form,' she said hurriedly when it looked as if he might go from her and over to the reception desk. *Tell him, tell him. He can't kill you while all these people are about.* 'I've got the keys,' she added, and quickly made for the lift area. Had she said keys, plural?

Thankfully there were other people going up with them in the lift. Then the lift doors opened, and she stepped out—and so too did Thomson. She went along to her room—he went with her. She stopped outside her door—and knew she could delay telling him the glad news no longer. Especially when, her key already inserted in the door lock, Thomson waited for her to open the door, and held out his hand for his key. She turned to face him.

'The thing is…' she began. His eyes narrowed—oh, grief, he knew something he wasn't going to like was coming.

'The thing is?' he prompted grimly when her words seemed to have got stuck.

'I gave your room away!' she said in one blurted-out mouthful.

He stared at her. Disbelievingly, Thomson just stood and stared at her. A second ticked by, and then another, and when his voice came it was dangerously quiet. 'You did—what?'

She was going to have to repeat it. 'I—er—gave your room away,' she managed bravely.

For perhaps another three seconds Thomson still continued to stare at her as if he just couldn't believe his hearing. Then, without wasting words, he was moving her to one side, and was turning the key in the door, opening up the room, and stepping inside.

'What…?' she gasped, following him in, her eyes taking in the chair, the table, the double bed.

He turned and looked down on her from his lofty height. 'Correction,' he stated. 'You gave *your* room away.'

'Oh, come on, Thomson.' She was tired, and she knew he was; it had been a long day; she was too tired to 'Mr Wakefield' him anyway. 'You'd have done the same.'

'I wouldn't.'

'There was this elderly couple—she'd just had her hip done. They offered her the office chair… You'd love the office chair. You could work all ni…'

He was not even tempted, she could tell. 'I'm having that bed,' he butted in.

'No, you're not! I am!' she insisted—and didn't like at all the way when, looking testily at her, a gleam of something other than irritability suddenly entered his eyes.

He transferred his gaze from her to the double bed, then back to her again, and his glance was definitely mocking, she realised when he suggested silkily, 'We *could* always share it, I suppose.' And Yancie wanted to hit him.

'You toad!' she berated her employer. 'You know what you can do to me, and how I don't want you to.'

He smiled an insincere smile, and she knew then that that was precisely why he'd made the offer to share—because he knew that she would never take him up on it. Not that he would again kiss her the way he had before. Well, she certainly wasn't going to ask him ever again for a goodnight kiss.

But she could be as crafty as him. 'If you insist, I'll go as far as sharing the room with you,' she called his bluff.

'No way!' he snapped curtly, as she had thought having no intention of sharing either bed or room—but oddly that made her angry suddenly.

'I'm not likely to want to have my wicked way with you!' she snapped.

He didn't answer for some seconds but was obviously weighing up his options. He must know, Yancie was positive, how the hotel was cram full with unexpected guests, and the possibility of getting a room elsewhere—should one care to go out again into the dreary, cheerless night—hopeless.

His mind was made up, apparently. 'You start anything and I'll sack you!' he threatened nastily—and Yancie's emotions were in an uproar.

She had only meant to call his bluff—but he had accepted! But—that aside—it made her furious that he should remind her she had been the one to start 'things' the last time. 'You should be so lucky!' she erupted, and thought for one weird moment that he was going to burst out laughing. Must be the weather affecting my brain terminals, she decided a moment later, because he was more glaring at her than laughing.

And then, as Thomson went and put his briefcase down on the table, Yancie all at once realised that—oh, heavens—she must have just agreed to share the room with him. She put her brain into overdrive mode. Her bluff to call his bluff by offering to share the room with him hadn't worked! While he'd initially decided it was out of the question, somehow she had talked him into changing his mind. Oh, crumbs!

While Yancie wasn't thrilled with the arrangement, she accepted that perhaps it was the only logical thing to do. But, while she felt that she knew enough of him to know she could just as well be sleeping on the planet Mars for all he was likely to come closer than he had to that night, she also felt it important that they get everything else settled here and now. Number one being that if anybody was going to have that double bed it was going to be her, not him. She looked at the one dumpy little chair in the room—if he thought she was going to sleep in that while he had the bed, did he have another think coming.

'Actually, Thomson—' she attracted his attention, wishing she'd missed off the 'Thomson,' but too late now '—I asked at Reception about dinner—but apparently they've had a run on food and there isn't any left.' She lied nicely. 'But I could swap you the bed for a cheese sandwich if you like?'

He studied her for long seconds. Then, 'Done,' he said, and, suddenly awash with guilt, Yancie gained the impression that Thomson had intended she should have the bed anyway.

She looked away from him, finding the bedside phone of much interest. 'They'll probably have handed out all the spare blankets too,' she said. 'It might be an idea to bring the car rug from the boot.'

'Anything else?'

Was he being sarcastic? She rather thought he was. 'Don't forget to ring your mother!' she snapped, and went storming off to the bathroom, certain that was a hastily smothered laugh that followed her. No wonder she hated him.

She rinsed her face and, for something to do, cleaned her teeth as well, and was soon in love with him again, hate having small chance of staying around for long when she loved him so much.

She went and listened at the door; all seemed silent in the next room. She opened the door and went in. Thomson wasn't there. No doubt he'd gone to get the car rug, and possibly to drown his sorrows with the rest of the herd at the bar.

Yancie took the sandwiches from her bag, opened one packet and ate a sandwich, leaving a packet and a half for him. She looked at her watch, and could hardly believe that it was half past nine already. She'd better ring home.

'You're fog-bound?' Fennia guessed when Yancie told her she wouldn't be home that night so not to worry. 'You stay where you are; with luck, it will be clear by the morning.'

Yancie rang off, hoping Fennia was right. She didn't know how she was going to get through one night sharing a room with Thomson; to have to share the room with him for a second night was unthinkable.

Where was he? It didn't take all that long to collect a car rug, did it? An abrupt and unwanted notion suddenly occurred to her. Oh, my giddy aunt, supposing, just supposing, he took it into his head to take a look around! Just supposing he took a look at the dining room. Oh, grief, he could, at this very moment, be having his dinner. In which case when he came back he might very well tell her she could keep her sandwiches; the deal was off, the bed his.

Possession, she decided, was nine-tenths of the law. She glanced about, and realised she couldn't lock him out because he had the room key with him. It would be undignified, as well as unfair, to put a chair under the door. She went for possession.

Hurriedly she cleaned her teeth again, took off her skirt and jacket and hung them up, briefly contemplated sleeping in her shirt, but decided against it, and hung that up too. She hadn't got a fresh shirt for tomorrow as it was—how much more rumpled her shirt was going to be if she slept in it. Besides, aggressive or kind, whatever Thomson's mood, she instinctively knew that it just wasn't in his nature to take advantage of her. She dispensed with her bra too, but because she drew the line at going to bed totally naked she opted to stay with her briefs. They were only bits of lace; she'd rinse them through in the morning; they'd soon dry.

She heard the sound of the lift, and dived into bed—and out again to put out the main light, and dived for the bed again. Then discovered she needn't have bothered for she realised it wasn't Thomson but, as voices neared and passed the door, a couple of other people staying in the hotel.

Yancie tried to sleep but couldn't. She felt too on edge. And when, the time nearing midnight, Thomson did return, her heart started to pound so resoundingly she thought he might hear it.

He didn't put on the light and Yancie, hearing him moving about, was suddenly conscience-stricken. He was so tall, and that chair was so small. Had she been in any way decently clad, she felt then that she would have got out of the bed and told him that he could have the bed. Modestly, however, and an unexpected feeling of shyness at the intimacy of the situation, kept her where she was.

Eventually the only noise to be heard was the occasional creak of the chair as Thomson adjusted his position. Yancie studied the line of light coming under the door from the hall and, her eyes quite well accustomed to the darkness, the room consequently seemed to lighten.

She grew sleepy and closed her eyes, and drifted into a light sleep somewhere around two in the morning. She was awake again at three, but it was not the creaking of the chair that awakened her, but the feel of Thomson, plainly having had enough of trying to get comfortable, coming to lie down on top of the bed beside her.

She was not alarmed, but glad. It was an obvious solution. She felt like telling him so, but thought better of it. She had an idea he'd probably leave the bed early so that she would be none the wiser.

It was strange, she mused, but she would have thought she would be furious to be sharing her bed with him—albeit she was the only one beneath the covers—but, in fact, she wasn't. Actually she felt more concerned for him than furious—concerned because the car rug wasn't making much of a job of covering him, and his bare feet were sticking out from under it.

She was still worrying about his feet when she fell asleep again. She didn't wake up again until, ploughing through her stirring brain, she suddenly became aware of a bare leg against her own—a leg that wasn't hers!

She jerked awake to find dawn was breaking and that the leg wasn't the only thing that was bare. She was sharing the bed with a man who had on about as much clothing as she had.

From stirring to wakefulness, she flew straight to agitated panic. Thomson's naked chest was against her left breast, his face so close to hers she could have kissed it. Though her inclination just then was more to bite it than kiss it.

She gave him a gigantic shove—and as she struggled to sit up, taking the duvet with her, he became awake on the instant, awake and alert. 'How *could* you?' she shrieked.

Thomson sat up too. She had the benefit of most of the duvet, and the sight of his naked broad shoulders and naked hair-roughened chest did nothing for her agitations. 'I didn't know I had,' were his first words.

'Don't get clever with me!' she charged; if he was trying to be amusing she just wasn't in the mood for it. 'You know what I mean—how dare you get under the bedcovers with me?'

'Ah!' he drawled, and then she realised he was too sharp for her. 'You knew I'd had enough of the chair and had to stretch out? You knew I'd joined you on the bed?'

She wasn't sure there wasn't a hint of kindness there—she was in no mood for that either. 'You didn't have to get *into* it!' she raged, wanting to push him furiously out of it, but not totally certain that he *was* wearing anything.

'Oh, put your chaste outrage away!' Thomson ordered bluntly. 'The central heating went off. I was half asleep, half frozen.' There was not a scrap of kindness in his tone when he went on to say, 'Do you honestly think that after our last amorous excursion I'd choose to repeat that non-event?'

Non-event! Her awakening! How she stopped herself from thumping him then she didn't know. Toad? He was worse than that! 'Fog or no fog,' she snapped, 'I'm going back the minute I'm dressed.' If he was about to say that went double for him, Yancie wasn't waiting to hear.

Wrenching the duvet the rest of the way off him, she made a cape of it and, turning all at the same time, she left the bed and went storming to the bathroom. Tears sprang to her eyes; she swallowed them back. She never used to be so emotional. She didn't want to be emotional. She didn't want to be in love. Being in love hurt. And making love to her was a non-event! Those intimate moments when she'd shared more of herself with him than any man had been a non-event! That awakening to how she felt, how she could feel, how she was her and not her mother—had been a non-event!

Yancie sat down on a bathroom stool with the duvet wrapped around her and hoped he froze. Though knowing him, without a cover to bless himself with, he was probably getting dressed and going to look for a cup of coffee. She could murder a cup herself.

It seriously crossed her mind to get dressed and get to the Jaguar and take off and leave Thomson stranded. Heaven alone knew where they were—she didn't. There was only one thing wrong with that—well, two, actually. One, Mr-non-event-never-again-Wakefield out there had the wretched car key. Two, if she did leave him stranded, it was a foregone conclusion she would lose her job. And, even though she was not thinking very kindly of him just then, she still wanted to keep her job. It was rare that she saw him, but she did sometimes, and she just couldn't face risking never seeing him again.

She got up and angrily shot the stiff bolt home on the bathroom door. Car key he might have, but he wasn't having the bathroom. The problem was, it was a bit boring sitting here doing nothing.

Yancie rinsed through her briefs, got most of the excess moisture out with a towel, and finished the drying process by use of the hairdryer attached to the bathroom wall. She felt like being perverse, and purely because she was positive, weather permitting or not, that Thomson would want to be on the road as soon as possible she decided she was no longer in a hurry.

She heard a sound like a door slamming to, and felt fairly confident that was the door to the room. She felt confident enough anyhow, though still with the security of the duvet around her, to unbolt the bathroom door and peer out. Good. T. Wakefield esquire had gone to breakfast.

Yancie went back inside the bathroom again, bolted the door and ran a bath. She had time, she decided, for a good long wallow. And, even if she hadn't, even if sir had merely gone to check road conditions and wasn't going to bother with breakfast, she was still going to enjoy her bath.

Yancie had her wallow, and found when she got out of the tub and patted herself dry that her long soak had calmed her. She was even slightly amazed that she could have been so mutinous. Hurt had done that to her. Since

falling in love, she'd experienced so many differing
emotions.

Never had she used to tell such whoppers either. Love
had made a liar of her. Not that she would ever lie to
Thomson over any large issue, so perhaps her small fibs
weren't so bad. Perhaps as long as they didn't hurt him
they didn't count.

Yancie knew for certain that she never wanted to hurt
him, and was just resolving that she'd be good from now
on when—shocking her so much she was like a startled
rabbit, incapable of movement—the bathroom door suddenly opened, and Thomson stood there. He was bare-
chested, but trouser-clad, and had obviously come in to
take a shower.

'I locked the door!' she shrieked. Where was the
towel?

While at the same time, his eyes staring as if hypno-
tised by her slender but curvaceous, long-legged body,
Thomson hurriedly started, 'You weren't around—I
thought you'd gone to breakfast.'

Panicking wildly, the towel back on the rail two yards
away, Yancie vaguely registered Thomson knew that the
hotel hadn't run out of food, and equally vaguely supposed that she had appropriated the bathroom long
enough to have bathed ten times over, so he could be
forgiven for supposing she had now vacated it.

But, suddenly and speedily, she was on the move, too
late now to fret that the door bolt couldn't have been so
far rammed home as it should have been. Yancie went
to dash past him, found the duvet had slipped off the
bathroom stool, and all at once, while trying to avoid
coming into contact with Thomson, she found she was
treading duvet.

'Ooh!' she cried, and 'Oh,' she wailed as the duvet

suddenly turned into an octopus that refused to let her go—and the next she knew she was falling.

She never got to hit the floor, though, because Thomson's arms shot out and he caught her, holding her while she tried desperately to get her balance. She clung onto him, her arms clutching at his arms, his shoulders—then, startled, she stopped treading the duvet and became aware of nothing except that he had one arm around her holding her upright, while his other hand was near enough holding her naked left buttock.

'Thomson!' she gasped, and realised from the shaken kind of look of him that he had just become aware of the same thing.

'Yancie,' he said in a strangled kind of way, and as if he could do nothing about it, and Yancie knew that she certainly couldn't as his head came down, so she turned her face up to meet him. And, as their lips met, nothing else seemed to matter.

It was a beautiful kiss, and Yancie wanted more. But Thomson was attempting to put some daylight between their two bodies. Yancie did her best to back away from him—but she felt hungry for his kisses.

'This is a nightmare,' he said, his voice hoarse, not like his usual tone at all.

She wanted to help, but how? 'I—don't know what to do,' she mourned huskily.

She saw him swallow, saw him try for a light note as he replied, 'I trust you aren't inviting me to show you.'

'I didn't mean that!' she strove to find the same light note—but missed by a mile.

'I know,' he said gently, and sent her such a wonderful smile, her legs almost buckled. He looked down into her upturned face. 'I should let you go,' he seemed to be talking more to himself than her. 'But...'

'But?' Yancie asked, her eyes on him, his mouth, the mouth she wanted to feel again. And, as his head came down again, so she did, and it was so heavenly she could have wept.

She wanted to cry his name from the pure ecstasy of it. But he was kissing her again, one hand caressing over her naked behind, and she was going light-headed from the pleasure of it.

He kissed her throat, and she placed her arms around him, holding him to her, her naked breasts against his bare chest. 'Thomson!' she cried, his name refusing to stay down.

'Dear Yancie,' he breathed, and she thrilled anew. Was she his dear? She kissed him, felt his caressing hands on her back, felt them caress round to her ribcage, then, with whispering tenderness, he captured her breasts. A sigh escaped her. The pink peaks of her breasts hardened incredibly under his touch, and as he brushed his palms lightly over the tips a fire went wild inside her.

She clutched onto him, unthinking, feeling only. She wanted him, oh, so much. Again he kissed her. Then he was capturing her breasts, moulding them, tenderly fondling, and Yancie was burning out of control.

When he bent his head and gently kissed the tip of first one breast and then the other, she soared to even higher heights of wanting. His mouth captured one breast, tormenting its wanting hardness with his tongue, while his other hand caressed and moulded over her other breast, over her body and down one thigh.

And Yancie didn't know quite where she was when, holding her a little way away from him, Thomson trailed kisses down her throat, over her breast.

'Oh, Thomson,' she murmured shakily when he held her to him again.

'I want you,' he told her, his voice thick in his throat.

'I—w-want you too,' she answered shakily—and guessed her nervousness must be showing, for suddenly he was gripping her arms tightly, and was deliberately putting an inch of daylight between their two bodies.

'This—er—' he broke off, then appeared to have got himself a little more together. 'This won't do, Yancie Dawkins,' he told her quietly, and Yancie, never wanting to leave his arms, just knew that their time of loving was over.

'It certainly won't,' she whispered, and, though she wanted to stay exactly where she was, from some unknown somewhere she actually found the strength to take a small step. Though, as Thomson started to take a pace back from her too, so she took a hasty grab at him, and when he looked at her she swallowed and, her colour high, began, 'I know, given that I haven't a stitch on, that I'm giving off all the signals that I haven't a shy bone in my body—but would you mind closing your eyes while I get out of here?'

That reluctant but wonderful smile of his came out and Yancie didn't want to go anywhere but back into his arms. But as he stood with his grey eyes gently holding hers, so he stretched out a hand and took a bath towel from the rail, shook it out and, with his eyes still on hers, wrapped the towel around her. Then he closed his eyes. 'Go, Yancie,' he said. 'While I can still let you.'

She wanted to stay. Wanted to kiss him—surely he would feel her touch and kiss her again? But, 'See you on the ice,' she gasped and, belatedly spying her briefs and hurriedly snatching them up as she went, she went quickly.

CHAPTER SEVEN

IT WAS Astra asking that afternoon if she was all right that warned Yancie she had better get her act together. Fennia had asked what was the matter just over a week ago.

'Yes, of c...' she began, and looked up to see that both her cousin Astra and cousin Fennia were observing her with a good deal of concern. And suddenly she couldn't bluff it out. 'Well, no, actually, I'm not,' she admitted, and her cousins urgently wanted to know what was wrong so that they could help. 'You can't help,' she told them, and confessed. 'I've done the stupidest thing—I've fallen for this man and he's so constantly in my head, there just isn't any room for anything else.'

'Oh, Yancie!' Fennia gasped.

'How does he feel?' Astra, the more practical one of the three, asked.

'Like—he doesn't want to know,' Yancie replied.

'I don't believe it!' Fennia exclaimed. 'To know you is to love you,' she added stoutly. And all three of them laughed.

'Tell *him* that,' Yancie said.

'Thomson Wakefield?' Astra asked.

'How did you work that out?' Yancie asked in amazement.

'There's something different about you when you come home after driving him,' Astra replied.

'Really? Well, I doubt I shall ever be driving him again,' Yancie said. He had driven as far as his home today. Then, as if their mind-blowing, intimate embrace had never happened, he'd bluntly instructed her to see to it that the Jaguar was returned to the firm's garage.

'Do you want to talk about it?' Fennia asked. Yancie shook her head, and loved her cousins the more that they didn't pry, but let her know that they were there for her at any time and in any place, Astra stating she was taking them out that evening. No man was worth staying in for on a Saturday night.

In actuality, Yancie would have preferred to stay home. She felt a need to be by herself, but Astra was right; she ought to be going out and setting about putting Thomson out of her head. But, how could she?

After her speedy exit from the bathroom she had hurriedly donned some clothes, attended to her light make-up and her hair. A hasty look out of the window had shown that, while weather conditions could have been better, they weren't as bad as they had been. Yancie had opted to wait for Thomson down in the hotel lounge.

She hadn't had to wait very long. But when she had been feeling all shy at the thought of seeing him again after their heated lovemaking it had been at once obvious from his cool expression that he was regretting what had happened.

'I'll drive,' he'd said, his tone even, but a hint of iron there that said, Don't argue.

Suit yourself, she'd fumed, hating him that he could put her on this emotional treadmill. There she had been, sitting there weaving cosy dreams where Thomson, when he joined her, he might suggest they met outside of work so that they might get to know each other a little better. But, forget it! He was physically attracted to her; she knew that much. But did he have to make it so painfully obvious that that was all it was—physical?

That his emotions were not otherwise affected? That, in fact, he didn't want to know her any better?

So why couldn't she stop thinking about the wretched man? It was for certain he wasn't wasting any time thinking about her.

In that, however, Yancie found she was wrong. It was around five, late that day, when she was drumming into her head how she was going to go out with Fennia and Astra that night, and how they were going to have a whale of a time, when the phone rang.

Fennia was in the bath, Astra was in her study; Yancie picked the phone up and said, 'Hello.'

'Thomson Wakefield,' he announced, and at the thought that he was ringing to ask for a date her mouth went dry. But, date? Forget it! 'I need a driver,' he went on, seemingly recognising her voice from that one word. 'Can you pick me up at seven?'

I'm afraid Yancie's out; she has a heavy date tonight, but I'll tell her you rang when I see her in the morning. She so nearly said it, but she loved the brute. 'No problem,' she answered, managing to keep her tone even. 'Where am I driving to? I mean, do I need to look up a route?'

'I'm attending a recital not far away; I'll give you directions when I see you.'

'Right,' she said—and hung up.

You're pathetic, Yancie, pathetic, she told herself, knowing that what she should have told him was, Drive yourself, and while you're at it you can have my resignation. Had not her emotions been involved, she would not have hesitated to do so. In fact the old Yancie would never have put up with so much. But this love she had for him had crept up on her and, while the old Yancie was still in there somewhere, love had, for the moment, debilitated her.

Fortunately there was more than one bathroom in the flat; Yancie went and showered and washed her hair and was dressed in a black trouser suit with a white silk shirt when she went to seek out her cousins. They were in the kitchen having a cup of tea.

'Er—I'll have to cancel tonight,' she opened.

'You've had a better offer?' Fennia asked.

'My boss rang—I've got to work,' Yancie explained.

'That's your new uniform, is it?' Astra grinned, knowing full well who her boss was.

Yancie had to laugh; so did Fennia. Yancie left the apartment. She was smiling again as it only then dawned on her that, for all Thomson had instructed her to return the Jaguar to the firm's garage, he must know that she hadn't done so yet. Just as he must know that she'd had no intention of doing so until Monday morning.

As she'd known they would, her insides started to play up as soon as she pulled up on his drive. She left the car and went to ring the doorbell of his home. She sent stern instructions to her facial muscles. Stay impassive. It might well be the housekeeper who answered the door, but it could equally well be Thomson, or even her ladyship, his mother!

The door opened and, looking splendid in dinner suit, crisp white shirt and bow-tie, Thomson stood there—and her heart fluttered crazily to see him.

He seemed a little taken aback to see her, she thought, but as his glance travelled over her, taking in her silk shirt, her long length of leg in her expensive trouser suit, Yancie realised that he was only taken aback because he had expected her to be dressed in the same fashion as when he had last seen her.

'My uniforms are at the cleaners,' she lied. Her mother was right; her uniform was drab.

'Shall we get on?' he ignored her lie—but very nearly poleaxed Yancie when he added, 'I have to collect my date, first.'

Yancie turned abruptly about so he shouldn't see her expression. She felt sick at heart, sick to her stomach, and was never more glad of her pride. Because it was pride, and pride alone, that got her through the next few minutes, and saved her from either crumpling there and then, or telling him he could drive himself, that she'd had it with him.

Yancie felt even sicker when his date turned out to be an elegant, sophisticated woman of about thirty or so. While she was not beautiful in the accepted sense, she had a certain charm Yancie could see some men might care for. Clearly Thomson Wakefield was one of them.

'It's very good of you to give up your Saturday evening to drive us,' she addressed Yancie from the rear, to Yancie's mind sitting much too close to Thomson.

Charm or condescension? 'Mr Wakefield caught me when I'd got nothing on,' Yancie replied, adding, 'Madam,' for the sheer hell of it. And, ignoring the cold look in Thomson's eyes as their eyes clashed in the rearview mirror, she started to grow angry with the pair of them. How dared this Julia-whatever-her-name-was patronise her? How dared Thomson—? Suddenly she was furious with him. He of the 'Go, Yancie. While I can still let you' that morning when, naked, she'd stood in the circle of his arms. He had known about—and had probably looked forward to—his date with *Julia* that night!

Following his directions, Yancie turned into the drive of a large manor house. There were many other smart cars parked in the drive. At first it pleased Yancie when she saw at once that she wouldn't be able to park in front of the house, that position already taken. It was a cold night; it wouldn't hurt *Julia* to walk a bit, to Yancie's way of thinking. Though when she had a sudden and unwanted vision of the woman hanging onto Thomson's arm as they walked up the drive Yancie decided to drive on and for a few seconds double park at the front door.

She stopped the car and heard Thomson's date voice the opinion that the recital and following supper would probably end at about eleven. He got out and went round to the passenger door to open it for her—jealously gave a vicious nip, and as far as Yancie was concerned the woman could break a leg before she'd get out and open the door for her. Having closed the passenger door, Thomson came to the driver's door, but whatever it was he had to say Yancie wasn't interested. She was off, away down the drive.

An hour later she'd cooled down sufficiently to go back again. That in itself had been a tussle. For her money, Thomson and his date could walk home. But they wouldn't, of course. There would always be someone around to give them a lift—and what would she have achieved, apart from losing her job? Nothing, except that she had given Thomson the idea that she had been upset about something. Bubbles to that!

Yancie found a parking spot and went for a stroll around. It was a bitterly cold night, so it wasn't much of a stroll. She did, however, notice, on walking by a Rolls-Royce, that there was a chauffeur's peaked cap on the front seat.

She had already decided that she wasn't going to go back to the car and sit there freezing to death until the

function was over. That clinched it. She'd go where all
good chauffeurs went on a bitterly cold night.

In actual fact, she found there were only three of them
when she made it to the kitchen. Mick, Jerry and her,
all the other guests—teetotallers or license-riskers, obviously—opting to drive themselves.

'You must be starved,' the housekeeper said, after a
while, when Yancie had explained who she was. 'I'll
just get this food sent up, and then you can have your
supper.'

It wasn't a bad life, being a driver, Yancie reckoned,
having dined on venison pie, duchesse potatoes, and a
cranberry and red cabbage mix. Afterwards, as they sat
at a table in a corner and Jerry got out a pack of cards,
Yancie found there were still some considerable gaps in
her education.

They had been playing cards for about an hour when
Mick volunteered, 'You're all right, Yancie. I thought
you might be a bit stuck-up when I heard your plummy
accent. But—you're all right.'

'Thanks,' she accepted his compliment. 'You're all
right too.'

An hour after that and one of the housekeeper's as-
sistants came in to say people were about to leave. 'See
you, Mick. See you, Yancie,' said Jerry, abandoning the
game.

It was a signal for the three of them to get back to
their vehicles. Yancie was behind the steering wheel
when Thomson and his date of the evening came out.
Yancie considered he was strong enough to open the
door for Julia—she wasn't moving, that was for sure.

'You've got the car warmed for us,' Julia observed
pleasantly, as Yancie moved off. 'I do hope you weren't
waiting outside all this while.'

'Oh, no,' Yancie answered pleasantly. 'I've been playing poker in the kitchen with some of the boys.'

Yancie heard a strangled sort of cough from her employer, hoped it was flu, and felt like saying as much—how *dare* he take somebody else out and have the nerve to ask her to drive him? But she wasn't speaking to him.

Which, sadly, didn't seem to affect him one iota. In fact he didn't even notice. But, when she was determined she wasn't going to utter so much as a word to him, she found, when they pulled up outside Julia's home, that her wayward tongue was getting away from her.

He had just helped his date out of the car, but poked his head back in. Though, before he could say what it was he had to say, Yancie heard herself enquire, 'Do you wish me to wait, sir?' Had she added, Or are you staying the night? it couldn't, she knew have been more obvious.

'Wait!' he snarled, and escorted his female inside the building.

As Yancie tormented herself by visualising Thomson taking the woman in his arms, so she almost took off and left him stranded there. Only a last-minute notion that he might yet decide to stay the night if he had no transport home kept Yancie where she was.

It felt as if a ton lead weight had been taken off her when, in next to no time, she saw Thomson coming out of the building. If he had kissed the wretched woman, then there'd been no time for him to make a meal of it.

Yancie decided she didn't want to think of him kissing somebody else, and the moment he was in the car she started it up and put her foot down. 'Watch the road conditions!' ordered a voice from the back.

The road conditions were icy and treacherous, and finding that Thomson was right and that she needed to concentrate totally on her driving gave Yancie little time in the next few miles to think of anything but the hazards presenting themselves as the night grew colder and colder.

They were in open country approaching a T-junction when Yancie was starting to think better of Thomson in that when she had been expecting that at any minute he would tell her to pull over, that he was driving, he had not.

It was about all she remembered, because a split second either way and they would have been all right. But, with abominable timing, they were passing the junction just as another car was going into a skid as it tried to come to a halt. It came hurtling at them—and there wasn't a thing she could possibly do to stop it. *'Thomson!'* she cried his name. If he said anything, she didn't hear it—in fact she didn't hear anything again for quite some while.

Her head hurt. Yancie came to, to find that she was in hospital. 'That's better,' a gentle, kindly voice soothed, and Yancie opened her eyes to find a nurse bending over her, having just finished sponging her face.

'What...?' Her head felt muzzy. 'Where...?' she tried again.

'You'll be all right,' the nurse reassured her. 'You're in hospital. You were in a car accident, but you've been extremely lucky. You've been concussed and have bruising and shock, but you're otherwise okay. You're going to be fine.'

'Wh...?' Yancie broke off. She had been driving. 'Thomson!' she exclaimed in panic. 'Thomson, where is he? Is he...?' Fear paralysed her. Her voice rose. 'Where is he? What...?' If he was dead, she wanted to die too.

But Thomson wasn't dead. Though he had not come out of the accident as well as her. They had both been brought to the same hospital, but he was unconscious still and was being nursed in the intensive care unit.

Yancie wanted to see him and vague promises were made that someone would take her to him, but nobody did. In fact, it wasn't until the next day, when she was allowed out of bed for the first time, that she managed to see him—courtesy of her two cousins.

She'd had a constant stream of visitors before and after she had regained consciousness, but Yancie's agitation over Thomson would not be held down any longer. Her mother had been to see her. Ralph, her aunt Delia and cousin Greville had just left when Astra and Fennia came again to visit.

'I've got to see Thomson,' Yancie fretted. 'Have you any idea where the intensive care unit is in this place?'

'I'll go and find out,' Fennia volunteered, and sped off.

Yancie somewhat shakily got to her feet. Everything hurt, but that did not concern her. 'I'm going to need you to lean on to get there,' she said to Astra.

'Hang on there for a minute,' Astra bade her, and disappeared, to return pushing a wheelchair. 'We're going to have to be quick,' she said, helping Yancie into it. 'I pinched it from outside the X-ray department.'

Just then Fennia came back to say she had enquired but only close family were being allowed to see Thomson. Between them Fennia and Astra wheeled Yancie to the intensive care unit. As they got there so a nurse was just coming through the double doors.

'This is Yancie Dawkins, a very close friend of Mr Thomson Wakefield. She has to see him,' Fennia announced.

The senior nurse surveyed the trio, with a professional eye on the pink silk-robe-clad pale figure in the wheel-chair. 'One minute,' she said after a moment, and, taking hold of the wheelchair, she ordered, 'You two stay here.'

Had Yancie had a smile in her she might have spared one for the nurse. But she was too anxious about Thomson to have a smile for anyone as the nurse wheeled her to where he lay, and where another nurse was on constant alert.

Yancie's heart turned over when she saw Thomson. A sheet pulled up to just above his waist was his only covering, while wires and tubes were attached to him, and monitors beat out a steady rhythm.

Tears threatened to choke her as Yancie stretched out her hand to gently touch the back of his hand as it lay on top of the sheet. Yancie covered his hand, and, able to see for herself that he was in a critical condition, she willed him to live.

'That's three minutes,' the nurse whispered to her, and Yancie looked at her, a question there in her distressed blue eyes. 'He's a fighter,' was the best the nurse would answer and, as Yancie took a last look at him, she turned her and wheeled her back to where Fennia and Astra were waiting.

The next few days were a total nightmare for Yancie. She wouldn't cry—to do so would mean she was ready to accept that there might be some doubt that Thomson would recover, and she wasn't going to have that. He would get better, he would, he would.

Yancie saw him twice more in those few days, and also established a communication line through the kindness of his nurses who apprised her nurses with the latest information on him. His mother was a constant visitor, apparently, and Greville had managed to see him. But

Greville did not know of Yancie's feelings for Thomson, so he concentrated on being sure she knew that no blame was attached to her for the written-off Jaguar, more than on trying to convince her that the chairman of the company would be all right.

'It wasn't your fault,' Greville assured her, when all she could remember was Thomson getting back in the car after seeing his date to her door. After that, it was all a complete blank. 'The other chap came out of it with nothing more than a broken arm, by the way.' Yancie did know, having thought to enquire. Greville continued, 'He may get prosecuted for driving without due care, but you've got nothing to worry about.'

Only Thomson. And her worry over him was driving her demented. And then he started to improve. Nicola Stewart, the nurse who had been with her when she had just rejoined the world, came back from her lunch break one afternoon to say Thomson had opened his eyes and, while still sedated, had regained consciousness and was back in the land of the living. Yancie very nearly cried then.

'May I see him?'

'You'll get me shot.'

'You don't have to take me. I'm getting stronger by the day, and the exercise will do me good. Dr Jordon was talking about the possibility of me going home on Friday—so I must be up to it.'

'You'll have to come back for physiotherapy for that shoulder,' Nicola Stewart began. Then, caving in, she said, 'You'd better make a dash for it round about tea-time when everyone will be busy.'

From what Yancie had seen there was never a time when the hospital staff weren't busy. But she wasn't arguing, and waited in a fever of impatience, glad for once not to have any visitors. Then, having taken a shower, brushed her hair and put some lipstick on, she made her 'casual' way along the hospital corridors.

She looked through the glass doors of the intensive care ward, and her heart went into her mouth when she saw that the bed Thomson had used was now occupied by somebody else.

She controlled her initial panic, reasoning that if he was starting to get better, even though he was still sedated, he had probably been moved to a side ward. Yancie was too anxious to see him to give up now. She pulled the edges of her silk dressing gown closer around her, and slowly, because she still ached all over, she went looking for him.

Yancie found him not too far away. She opened a door two doors down from Intensive Care, and there, allowed one pillow this time, he lay. He was awake—and Yancie didn't know what to say.

She went closer to the bed. 'I suppose this puts paid to my driving career,' was what she did say—and joy, utter joy, filled her heart when he found a smile for her.

'Yancie!' he exclaimed, uttering her name, and, albeit he appeared to be infinitely weary, she felt he seemed pleased to see her. She went closer—and needed the chair that was pulled up to the bed when he stretched out a hand to her. She sat down quickly and gave him her hand. 'They said you were all right,' he said, just the effort of talking seeming to drain him of energy. 'But...'

'I'm fine,' she assured him swiftly, while finding it incredible that in the short time he'd been conscious he must have asked about her. But she was more concerned then that he hang onto what reserves of strength he had.

He smiled, gripping her hand. She wanted to kiss him,

to hold him safe and kiss his dear head, and felt choked
to the core of her being when he teased, 'And what mischief have you been up to today—given that it looks as
though you've given your warders the slip?'

Yancie laughed—she guessed her dressing gown had
given her away. 'I haven't been up to any mischief,' she
said softly, loving him, loving this way he was being
with her. 'I promise,' she added, knowing as his eyelids
started to droop that it would be more health-giving to
him if she left now and let him sleep.

So, although she would by far have much preferred
to stay exactly where she was, she started to get to her
feet. Though she sat down heavily when his eyes opened
again, and, every bit as if he was fighting with all he
had to beat off the effects of the sedation that had been
administered, he requested, 'Promise me something
else.'

'Anything,' she replied, and meant it.

He gave her hand a faint squeeze. 'Promise me,
Yancie Dawkins, that you'll marry me?' he said.

Yancie sat rooted, her mouth fallen open, and was still
not believing what she thought she had heard when his
fight against his medication failed, and his eyelids
drooped once again, and he went to sleep.

Feeling stunned, Yancie just sat there holding his
hand. He *had* said it; he had. She knew he had. 'Promise
me, Yancie Dawkins, that you'll marry me', he had said.
He'd proposed! Incredibly, Thomson had proposed!
Yancie was still in stunned shock when—the nursing
staff still keeping a strict eye on him, it seemed—a nurse
came in and Yancie knew her visit with him was over.

His proposal and the fact that he looked so much better stayed with Yancie for the rest of that day. Though
when Fennia and Astra came to visit her that evening

she found she couldn't tell them of it. Instead she asked
them to bring her some clothes in.

'You're thinking of going over the wall?' Astra queried, having taken home the clothes Yancie had been
wearing.

'They're letting me out the day after tomorrow. But
I've had enough of nightwear,' Yancie answered.

'I'll drop some stuff off on my way to work in the
morning,' Fennia promised.

Yancie couldn't sleep that night for thinking of what
Thomson had asked. And, while part of her denied his
proposal had any meaning, she just couldn't believe he
would ever say something like that and not mean it. *He
was drowsy, remember.* Yes, but he had known it was
her he was speaking to. Must have done. Yancie
Dawkins, he'd called her. 'Promise me, Yancie
Dawkins, that you'll marry me?' Excitement surged up
in her. Did he love her; dared she hope? She couldn't
wait to see him tomorrow.

Fennia dropped by in the morning with some clothes
for her, as she'd said she would. 'Anything you need
when I come in tonight?' she asked before she dashed
off to her nursery work.

'I have everything,' Yancie smiled, and as Fennia
went on her way Yancie couldn't help but wonder, and
hope, Had she? If it was true and Thomson did want to
marry her, did love her, she would not want for anything
else.

Fennia had brought Yancie one of her very favourite
dresses—a very fine wool affair in a most gorgeous
shade of blue. Yancie showered and dressed and waited
as long as she possibly could before she slipped along
the corridors.

She was nearing the side room where she had seen

Thomson yesterday, when all her hopes were sent crashing. Mrs Wakefield was just coming out of his room. Yancie saw that Thomson's mother had recognised her and knew that she wasn't thrilled to see her when, coming only a little away from the door, she blocked her progress.

'Haven't you done enough?' she challenged viperishly.

'The accident wasn't my fault,' Yancie pointed out reasonably.

'What are you doing here?'

Honestly! 'I've come to see Thomson,' Yancie answered—grief, if all her dreams came true, this dragon was going to be her mother-in-law!

'Thomson, is it?' Mrs Wakefield challenged, in Yancie's view clearly having been feasting on the churlish tart again. '*Mr Wakefield*,' the woman went on heavily, 'has no wish whatsoever to see you.'

'I think you'll find you're wrong there,' Yancie refused to give ground.

Mrs Wakefield cared not. 'The only persons my son wishes to see—' she ignored what Yancie had said '—are myself and his fiancée.'

Yancie went cold. 'H-his fiancée?' she questioned huskily, feeling staggered, and knowing it was showing. 'I—didn't know Thomson was engaged.'

'I can't think why you should imagine you have any right to know!' Mrs Wakefield said arrogantly.

Hope, stupid blind hope, began to surge upwards in Yancie again. Oh, heavens, could it be, dared she hope, that Thomson had just told his mother that he was getting married? True, he had fallen asleep yesterday before she'd had a chance to say yes, yes, a thousand times yes, but... 'When did...?'

'Not that it's any business of yours, but my son and Julia Herbert have been engaged for quite some months now.'

'I…' Yancie gasped, reeling, her colour draining away. Then pride, wonderful, face-saving pride, took a nip at her. 'Of course. Julia. I'm sure they'll both be very happy.' With that, and it took all her strength to stay physically upright, Yancie turned about and went back the way she had come.

She left hospital the next day. She had discovered through the nursing network that Thomson was off the critical list, and was expected to make a full recovery. That news warmed her heart, but it was the only joy she found.

Knowing that he was expected to make a full recovery did not stop her from worrying about him, however, and she picked up the phone several times in the following twenty-four hours to ring the hospital before putting it down again. He didn't care about her, and she was being silly.

Saturday afternoon had rolled around before, silly or not, she just had to give in to the compulsion to ring the hospital to find out how he was. 'Mr Wakefield was well enough to be moved,' she was informed by an efficient-sounding voice.

'He's gone home!' Yancie exclaimed; he wasn't well enough yet! He couldn't be.

'He won't be ready to go home for a week or two yet,' she was informed. 'Although, once he's on his feet, he should from then on make a speedy recovery.'

That was a relief. 'He's gone to another hospital?' Yancie realised. 'May I know which one?'

'I'm afraid I'm not at liberty to say.'

Yancie saw Mrs Wakefield's hand in that. She could

almost hear her giving the instructions not to give out
to anyone where he had transferred to—particularly not
to any company driver.

Yancie did find out where Thomson was, however.
Greville told her. He kept in touch, wanting to know
about her progress, and seemed to see it only as a normal
reaction—since she had been driving Thomson at the
time of the accident—that she would want to know about
him. It was a red-letter day when Greville told her
Thomson had been discharged from hospital.

As well as flowers from Kevin Veasey, Yancie had
received a host of lovely get-well cards from Wilf Fisher
and the other men in the transport department at work.
But when her bruised shoulder was healed enough for
her to go back to her driving duties Yancie had to give
serious thought to her future—did she want to go back?

She still needed paid employment; there was no doubt
about that. But could she face seeing Thomson again?
Face possibly driving him again? Well, you never knew;
they might be desperately short-handed one day and
Thomson would have to take the risk; though that accident had never been her fault anyhow.

But, while aching to see him again, what good would
it do? Could she bear to drive him knowing he was engaged and could be planning to marry Julia at any time?
She might even be called upon on some occasion to
drive both him and *her*.

Knives seemed to stick in her heart. That, she knew,
she couldn't take. Without giving herself time to think
further, Yancie rang Kevin Veasey—and resigned.

'You're sure?' he asked, adding, obviously not holding the written-off Jaguar against her, 'You don't want
to think about it for a while?' And, clearly assuming she
had lost her nerve after the accident, he assured her, 'I'm

sure, given time, that once you get behind the wheel
again...'

'You're very kind, Kevin. But I've decided to train
for a different career.'

She would too, she vowed—only not just yet.
Although her bruises had cleared up, she still felt mentally bruised, beaten—and needed some time.

Which she had in plenty. Between them Fennia and
Astra wouldn't allow her to do a thing domestically. And
days stretched endlessly before her. Days when she had
time to think. Too much time to think.

She half regretted her decision to leave Addison Kirk
when Greville told her a couple of weeks later that
Thomson had returned to work. She had given up all
chance of seeing him again. But she must be strong. To
make a clean break of it was the only way.

Yet that didn't stop her thinking about him. She went
over and over again her every meeting with him.
Recalled again that first meeting, remembered how she
had thought he didn't have a laugh in him, and then
recalled seeing him laugh.

Yancie knew she was spending too much time just
dwelling on his every word, his every look, his every
action, but she couldn't seem to stop. She didn't want
to love him, but she couldn't stop that either.

She recalled how passionately they had kissed. How
it had seemed then that they would make complete and
beautiful love with each other. And how he had been so
wonderful at her first hint of hesitancy.

He'd had too much common decency to attempt to
persuade her after understanding her hint of uncertainty,
even though he had probably known that her resistance
would have been a weak thing had he renewed his on-
slaught to her senses.

His innate decency, his integrity, was something else she loved about him. She'd heard him time enough on the car phone dealing with some business or other, or dictating some important correspondence to Veronica Taylor, and knew that his integrity was unshakeable.

She remembered the...

Yancie's thoughts suddenly ceased mid-flow. That word 'integrity' began to pound in her head. They just didn't come any more ethical than Thomson; she just knew it. Suddenly her heart, which had been a plodding muscle of late, started to race. Was she supposed to believe that once he left his office, once he put his business dealings aside, Thomson put his in-built integrity aside also?

She couldn't believe it, she realised. She could not. And yet that was what she had been believing. All these weeks she had trusted, believed what his mother had told her—that he was engaged to Julia Herbert and had been for some months now.

But, leaving alone that the men in the transport section were the biggest gossips she'd ever met, not one word had she heard about him being attached to anyone. Could she believe Thomson would forget totally and utterly that he had a fiancée when some other woman more or less invited him to kiss her?

Loud and strong the answer hammered back—no, he would not. Yancie pulled at the question every way she could. She had to work it out squarely and not arrive at the conclusions she wanted to arrive at purely because she could not take much more of this living in limbo.

He'd kissed her, she'd responded—oh, my, how she'd responded. But—he hadn't pushed her away, as a man engaged to someone else, a man with his integrity, would have. Thomson had instead kissed her again, many times. And, Yancie felt, would have made her his. Yet would he completely ignore the fact that some other woman was wearing his ring?

Had Julia been wearing his ring? Yancie couldn't remember seeing a ring on her finger; but then she couldn't remember not seeing one, either.

Yancie's stomach tied up in knots at the magnitude of her thoughts. If Thomson wasn't engaged to someone else, then he had every right to kiss where he pleased. Every right to ask someone else to marry him.

Yancie knew that she was not very good company for Astra and Fennia that night, and she went to bed early, to plough through the same thoughts over and over again.

But it was the not knowing that moved her to do something about it the next morning. Yancie was up early, checking through her wardrobe. She knew what she had to do. She felt nervous, shy, all churned up in her stomach—but she couldn't take another day of going around in the same not-knowing circles. She was going to have to go and see Thomson.

Of course he might have absolutely no recollection of asking her to marry him. He had been critically ill, remember. Well, she might not even mention that—but at least, if he had some memory of asking her to marry him, he was entitled to an answer. And what Yancie did remember was that she hadn't given him one.

Fortunately both her cousins went to work early—Yancie felt much too uptight to want to talk about this obsession that had taken her over with anyone but him.

She was wearing an elegant suit that had once fitted snugly but which, although still looking smart, now hung on her thinner frame as she made her way inside the Addison Kirk building.

She chose not to go to the reception desk—she was not in any mood to have her progress stopped before she'd made it as far as the lifts. But, having made it to the lifts, having got in and started to ascend, Yancie's insides started acting up with a vengeance.

Doubts, great clawing, scratching, spiteful doubts, started to go for her the moment she stepped out onto the floor where Thomson had his office. Don't be ridiculous, scorned the gremlin that had just jumped on her shoulder. Just because Thomson was totally honourable in his workplace, it didn't necessarily mean that he was the same in his relationships. Why, the world was littered with two-timing men who...

She reached his door and found she was half hoping he wasn't in. Didn't she know from personal experience that some days he didn't come into the office at all, but had a driver pick him up from his home and take him wherever his business happened to be?

Oh, please, let him be in! She felt a total mass of contradiction as, having no intention of calling first at his PA's office only to have Veronica Taylor tell her he was too busy to see her, Yancie reached for the handle of Thomson's office door.

She swallowed, gripping it hard, some part of her wanting to flee, her life seeming to depend on her staying and going in. Her last memory before the accident had been of Thomson getting into the Jaguar after he'd seen Julia Herbert to her door. He hadn't wasted any time about seeing her to that door, either, but was soon back, Yancie made herself remember. What sort of behaviour was that for a supposedly engaged man?

On that thought, Yancie gathered together all of her courage, opened the door and went in. Thomson was there. He looked up from his desk, plainly not expecting anyone. He was thinner too, she saw straight away, and her heart started to ache for all his suffering. But he was staring at her as if astounded by her nerve in barging into his office unannounced—as if she was the last person he expected to see. She wanted to speak, but her throat felt parched. 'H-how are you?' was what she managed for openers.

'I don't recall having an appointment with you!' he barked curtly, rapidly recovering from having appeared momentarily rocked.

Appointment! He really could be a swine when he wanted, she fumed; she was angry, not to mention a bundle of nerves into the bargain. Perhaps that was why, when she had half decided not to mention his proposal if he didn't remember it, she forgot totally what she had or had not decided, and snapped back bluntly, 'That's no way to speak to your fiancée!'

Her mouth fell open from the shock of the unintended words she had just hurled at him. But as Thomson, rising from his desk, stared back at her, his expression positively staggered, Yancie didn't know which of them was the more shocked. What she did know, though, was that this was the first he'd heard of it—or wanted to hear of it.

It was time, she realised, for her to get out of there!

CHAPTER EIGHT

IT WAS obvious to Yancie from Thomson's absolutely thunderstruck look that he had not the smallest recollection of ever having proposed to her. And, bearing in mind the strong medication he must have been receiving, she realised, belatedly, that she should never have mentioned it to him.

'I'm—sorry!' she gasped before he had uttered a word—and was on her way.

Unbelievably, however, Thomson had moved, and moved fast, and was at the door before her, his hand down by the door handle, preventing her from reaching for it.

There was a sharp look in his eyes she felt suddenly wary of. 'Tell me more,' he commanded.

No way! But he seemed pale. Had he just lost his colour from the shock of her claiming to be his future wife—as if that thought would make any man go pale—or had he been pale to start with?

'You haven't been well!' she exclaimed, fearful for his health.

'I was given a clean bill of health only yesterday.'

Yet, typically, he'd been at work before he'd been given the all-clear—probably been working from home before that. 'I shouldn't trouble you,' she said jerkily.

'You've been trouble from the day I met you,' he replied, his eyes on hers, searching, reading.

'Well, you would say that!' she attempted an offhand note that didn't quite come off—she didn't like the shrewd, alert look of him; he was clever, discerning; she knew that much about him. 'W-well, I'll be off; I just thought I'd pop in to see how you are.'

She didn't like at all, either, the speculative look that had come to his eyes. 'My drivers are doing it all the time,' he answered dryly, his eyes never leaving her face.

Pig! 'Well, you look all right to me!' she snapped, glad of a spurt of anger, but wishing he would come away from the door so she could go through it. 'Well, I'll love you and leave you,' she hinted, and could have groaned aloud that she had trotted out that trite little saying. She wanted to keep a mile away from that word 'love'. She shouldn't have come; she shouldn't, she shouldn't.

'No need to rush off,' Thomson stated calmly, at ease when she was feeling hot all over. 'Stay—have a cup of coffee,' he invited.

Coffee! 'This isn't a social call,' she blurted out in a rush. She needed to get out of there—and now.

'It isn't?'

'W-we were in an accident together,' she reminded him, even though she full well knew he needed no reminding.

He stood straight before her and while he continued to stare silently at her she would have given anything to know just what he was thinking, just what was going through his brain. Because she knew, too, that his waking brain was never dormant. His eyes fixed on hers, he seemed to draw a long breath, and then quietly, watchfully, he declared, 'I think there's more than an accident between us, Yancie.'

Oh, grief! Did he mean he knew that she loved him?

She couldn't bear it if he did. 'If you'll g-get out of the way,' she endeavoured again to get out of there.

But, again, he wasn't moving. 'It's not like you to be nervous,' he observed, still in that same quiet tone.

'N-nervous? Me! Pfff!' she denied swiftly, and made another attempt to get out of there before this all too perceptive man sifted out what she was nervous about. 'I must go—I'm sure you never have a minute to spare for unexpected callers.'

Her hint fell on stony ground. 'I've just made an exception.'

'Too kind!' *Oh, don't be snappy—you may never see him again.* That thought was so unbearable, Yancie burst into speech. 'You're thinner!' she said hurriedly, feeling more agitated than ever suddenly.

She wished at once she hadn't said it, because her remark brought his eyes from her face to skim over her shape, a much too speculative look in his grey eyes as he fixed them on her blue eyes once more, and quietly remarked, 'You don't appear to have put on a whole lot of weight, either.' And, acute assessment not in it, he said, 'Why is that, I wonder?'

'We've both b-been—er—unwell,' she supplied in an endeavour to put him off the scent—love had walked in; her appetite had walked out.

'How are you feeling now?' he enquired pleasantly.

Pretty desperate, actually. But his pleasant tone, plus the fact that he had accepted her answer without further question, caused her to drop her guard in her relief, and it was chattily that she answered, 'You mean how long have I been having these hallucinations?' The moment the question was out, she wanted it back. She had now gone from merely nervous and agitated to panic-stricken. She had been hoping that Thomson had forgotten her claim to be his fiancée but, with those words 'That's no way to speak to your fiancée!' clanging stridently away in her head all the while, she had just reminded him.

In all probability he had never forgotten it, she realised, but—was it too much to hope that those words were not clanging so loudly in his head; that he might not have a clue what she was meaning with her talk of hallucinations?

It *was* too much to hope for, she was very soon made aware. Because, whatever trauma Thomson had suffered from the accident, it had not impaired the quickness of his thinking, Yancie found. And he was right there with her when he questioned, 'To claim to be engaged to me, do I take it that I proposed?' He paused, and then very quickly added, 'And that you accepted?'

For all he seemed tense as he waited for her answer. Yancie knew that he was playing with her—and she didn't thank him for it. 'Oh, you proposed all right—but you're not engaged to *me*!' she answered snappily.

His eyes narrowed slightly. 'I make it my life's work to go around proposing to women?'

'According to your mother, you've been engaged to Julia Herbert for months!'

'Julia H...' Thomson stared at her disbelievingly. 'My mother told you I was engaged to Julia Herbert?' he questioned, seeming stunned. But, collecting himself, he caught a hold of Yancie's arm. 'I should have known that nothing is ever straightforward when it involves you, Yancie Dawkins,' he said at length. 'Come and take a seat, and you can tell me all about it.'

'You're busy,' she tried, but it seemed he'd got his determined hat on.

'Business can wait!' he said firmly. 'Things have been

going on here of which I know nothing!' And with that he led her over to the comfortable-looking sofa.

Yancie, by this time, was a trembling wreck. She had a feeling that what Thomson didn't know which he felt he should he resolutely found out. She wanted to flee, wanted to stay, wanted more time with him, even if it was just a mutual 'It's been nice working with you' kind of time. But he was urging her to be seated, and, truth to tell, she was feeling rather feeble in the leg department.

She saw a hint of a smile cross his features when she gave in and took a seat on the sofa, but noticed that he didn't turn his back on her, didn't take his eyes off her or give her a chance to dash for the door when he went to the intercom and told his PA, 'I'm with someone, Veronica. See to it I'm not disturbed, will you?'

Yancie stared at him. He needn't worry; she didn't feel capable just then of getting up and making a dive for the door. More so when Thomson came over and drew one of the easy chairs close up to her—and looked steadily into her nervous blue eyes.

'I didn't know you were so friendly with my mother,' he commented.

'I'm not!'

'And yet you say you know her well enough for her to impart details of my personal life.'

'I don't know her at all,' Yancie insisted. 'She was just there one of the times I came to see you in the hospital.'

'You came more than once?' he questioned sharply, that alert look in his eyes again.

Had he remembered her coming to see him that day? She couldn't ask. Yancie was all at once feeling on very shaky ground. She needed to get out of there, and with her pride intact. And yet she couldn't go. And, she discovered, when she had been able to lie to him in the past, now, with his eyes steady on hers, to lie to him was totally beyond her.

'I came several times,' she confessed, and felt her heart go a touch crazy that his breath seemed to catch and a warm kind of look came to his eyes. But she was fearful she was reading more into his every word, his every look than there actually was, so went on hurriedly, 'Well—we were both in the same hospital—though I doubt you'd have come to see me had you been the one who was mobile,' she added hurriedly. And was pleasantly contradicted for her trouble.

'Don't doubt it for a moment,' Thomson assured her. 'My first thought when I regained consciousness was you and how you'd fared.' *Well, don't read anything into that, Yancie. You were his employee, remember; naturally he'd...* 'I was still wired up to various contraptions when I knew I had to see for myself how you were.'

'You weren't well enough,' Yancie said softly, knowing she was in a meltdown situation again, even as she tried to rise above it.

'I threatened to come and find you, just the same,' he replied, shaking Yancie rigid.

'But—but you were all tubed up!' she exclaimed.

'Which is probably why, a short while before you escaped your warders, they zapped me with something guaranteed to keep me quiet,' he transfixed her by saying.

'You—you remember my visiting you that day?' The question wouldn't stay down this time as she clearly recalled how he'd teasingly spoken then of her warders.

'You were wearing a pink silk robe,' he answered, and Yancie swallowed on a suddenly dry throat.

'Do you—remember anything—else?' she asked jerkily, excusing, 'You had just been heavily sedated so I don't suppose...'

'I was fighting that sedation all the way,' he cut in, but he paused and, holding her eyes with his own, he said clearly, 'I can quite well remember that I asked you to marry me.'

Her heart wasn't merely pounding, it was thundering. She swallowed hard, and managed to find an uncaring smile as she replied, 'Well, in those circumstances, I'll do the honourable thing and not hold you to it.'

Thomson drew a long breath, and, leaning forward in his chair, he looked at her for long moments, and then plainly stated, 'I would regard that as a very great pity, Yancie.'

'Y-you—would?' Her voice had come out sounding all weak and feeble. Yancie took rapid steps to alter that. 'Just how many fiancées do you want, Mr Wakefield?' she asked a touch sharply.

'Only one. I'll have a word with my mother on the subject of her powers of invention.'

'Don't bother on my account.' *Invention?*

Thomson looked at her levelly. 'While I'm willing to concede there's a vast amount I don't know about you, I think I've learned enough to know that you wouldn't have come here to see me today without some good reason. And while, I might add, you took your time in getting here I'll tell you now that all Julia Herbert has ever been to me is a friend.'

'Your mother made the fiancée bit up?'

'She did,' he answered. And, just as though he could see that her head was having a hard time coping, he urged, 'Just take on board, Yancie, that I have never proposed marriage to anyone but you.'

Oh, my—her legs had gone weak again. 'Did you mean it?' She found enough nerve to ask, knowing she was just about going to die if he laughed his socks off.

He did not laugh. If anything, he seemed nervous suddenly, and that surprised her. But after a moment or two he manfully admitted, 'I took a long time getting there, a long time in accepting the feelings, thoughts, joy, that invaded my life on the day I met you.' He smiled and, leaning forward, he tenderly kissed her cheek. 'Oh, yes, dear Yancie,' he said softly as he pulled back and looked into her eyes. 'Oh, yes, I meant it.'

Yancie looked at him, tears welling up inside. He meant it! He meant it. Thomson had meant it when he had asked her to marry him. She wanted to throw herself into his arms. Wanted to hold her arms tight about him. But—she was nervous still. Nervous, and very unsure. 'Th-this has never happened to...' she broke off; she was saying too much! 'I think I'm in a bit of a panic,' she confessed, loved it when he smiled and gently caught a hold of her restless hands. His touch warmed her through and through and gave her the confidence she needed to enquire, albeit huskily, 'You spoke of feelings and things, on the day we met.'

'That day you crashed into my life,' he murmured, and Yancie could read nothing but encouragement in his eyes as he recollected the event.

'Leaving aside I didn't quite crash into you, though I concede it was a close thing,' she said, managing in her nervousness to find a smile, 'you weren't so benign that day.'

'Why would I be?' he countered. 'There was I in my work-filled world, a man who didn't have time for nonsense, and there you were, in a place where you shouldn't be—naturally—having very nearly caused an accident—and giving me a load of lip.'

'You could have dismissed me for that,' Yancie murmured.

'Which was the puzzling thing,' he said.

'Puzzling?'

'It was to me. I just couldn't think why I hadn't issued instructions for your department head to get rid of you.'

'You sent for me instead.'

'Fully intending to dismiss you myself,' he smiled.

Her heart was racing. Surely there was a tender look in his eyes for her! 'But you didn't dismiss me,' she reminded him, a little breathlessly.

'Oh, my dear, dear Yancie, how could I? You'd entered my life, crashed into it, and brightened up my dull world.'

She swallowed. 'I did?' she questioned chokily—his dear, dear Yancie? She started trembling anew.

'You did,' he replied. 'While I'm still wondering what on earth I am doing not only using my valuable time personally interviewing you—and prolonging that interview—I find that you're making me inwardly smile so much, my intention to dismiss you never got said...' Thomson broke off, paused, and then distinctly said, 'I realise now that you had started to get to me even then.'

'Oh,' she mumbled, wanting more, needing more, much, much more. 'What are you saying, Thomson?' She just couldn't hold back from asking. And, to her delight, discovered that he was in no mind to hold back. Not now.

For, fixing her with that steady gaze, perhaps reading in her beautiful blue eyes her nervousness, her need to know, he said, 'I'm saying, sweet, dear, often aggravat-

ing Yancie, that when I was a busy, work-oriented man
with no time for nonsense I got you as a driver, and my
world as I knew it started to fall apart.'

Yancie stared at him, her eyes huge. 'What did I do?'
she asked—and heard a whole list of what she had done.

Though first Thomson leaned forward and placed a
feather-light kiss to her mouth, and seemed reluctant to
pull back. But, having done so, he began, with a smile,
'You turned up late, took me on short cuts that turned
out to be the long way round—not to mention running
out of petrol while you were about it. You made me
laugh—in spite of me telling myself that I didn't find it
in the least amusing—you made me laugh. You beat me
up. Gave my hotel room away and expected me to sleep
in a chair. Got a fit of the giggles when...' he broke off,
then added, 'And life is so unutterably dull without you.'

Yancie swallowed hard. 'I'm a terrible person,' she
whispered shakenly.

Thomson gripped both her hands tightly in his, and,
looking deep into her eyes, said, 'So, is it any wonder
that I've—fallen in love with you?'

Her mouth fell open from the shock of hearing him
say what she so wanted to hear. 'Oh, Thomson!' she
gasped tremulously.

'It's all right, isn't it?' he asked quickly. 'Hell, I'm
so confident in the work I do—but this. I feel as shaky
as some schoolkid.'

'Yes, it's all right,' she told him quickly. 'It's fine. I
want you to love me.'

'You do?'

He still seemed tense, and hurriedly again Yancie replied, 'It's what I want more than anything.'

His eyes searched her face. 'You've lied to me before—you're not lying now?'

'Oh, Thomson, I'll never lie to you again!' she cried, feeling slightly astounded that he should need her reassurance.

'Then tell me truthfully—what are you feeling for me?' he promptly wanted to know.

And, when Yancie had always been a fairly confident person, suddenly, and quite ridiculously, she felt, experienced an overwhelming shyness to tell him of her love. 'I…' she tried, but didn't make it. She tried another tack. 'When you were in hospital and were so ill, I knew that if you died I wanted to die too.'

'Oh, my darling,' he said hoarsely, and, as if he couldn't sit merely holding her hands any longer, he moved to the sofa to be closer to her, thrilling her by taking her into his arms. 'Thank God you escaped with so few injuries.'

'You asked about me?'

'Repeatedly when you didn't come to see me again.'

'After you'd asked me to…' shyness gripped her again.

'After I'd asked you to marry me,' he finished for her.

'I came the very next day—only I bumped into your mother guarding the door.'

He shook his head, hardly crediting what she was telling him. 'I'd no idea that my mother had interfered. That you'd tried to visit me,' he owned. 'I found out from Greville that you were getting on so well they'd allowed you to go home. That you went home without bothering to stop by my hospital room to visit me again clearly meant, I thought, that my proposal meant nothing to you.'

'No!' she protested, and they just seemed to kiss quite naturally.

'Wonderful medicine,' Thomson breathed.

'You never thought to try and get in touch with me?' Yancie asked, not caring about anything any more. She was here with Thomson, the man she loved, the man who, incredibly, loved her.

'Would you, sweetheart? You hadn't come to see me again. Two days I waited, watching the door, my heart leaping every time it opened, hoping it would be you. I thought, when you didn't come, that I had your answer. After a few days of waiting I couldn't take any more— I switched hospitals.'

Her anguish for him sent her shyness flying. 'Oh, Thomson, I do so love you!' she cried—and as joy broke in him so Thomson gathered her close up to him once more. Held her close, and kissed her, held her, pulled back so he could read the truth in her face, in her eyes, and he kissed her again.

'When did you know?' he asked, holding her still, but seeming to want to know everything about her.

'I suspected it that night I was late picking you up, the night we ran out of petrol,' she began, feeling then she could tell him anything, so confessed, 'I'd been delivering a parcel to the mother of one of the mechanics. She lives in Derby.'

'Not too far away,' Thomson teased; oh, she did love him so. 'Even if you did get me all knotted up inside that you were late and might have had an accident.'

'You—were worried?' she asked, staggered.

'Going silently demented,' he owned. 'Later I had a chance to hold you safe in my arms. I knew you were getting to me in a big way when I felt I wanted to keep on holding you safe.'

'Back then!' she exclaimed.

'Before then, if I'm honest,' he answered.

'Oh, be honest, please,' she invited.

Thomson grinned, a wonderful grin. Her heart turned over. 'What can I tell you, Yancie mine? Shall I tell you how I tried to convince myself I had no interest in you—yet found you were in my head more and more?'

'Yes, please,' she sighed.

He laughed, kissed the top of her head, and went on, 'Even when I was telling myself it wouldn't do, thinking about you all the while, that I'd have another driver—other drivers had the wrong-shaped head, the wrong-shaped hands on the wheel. But even as I was telling myself that I'd be better off with a driver who wasn't impudent, with one who wouldn't lie to me, one who wouldn't cause me to get plastered in farmyard mud—I was having to face that other drivers didn't have the power to make me laugh—in spite of myself.'

'Did I do that?'

He nodded. 'Life has been so unbearably flat without you,' he revealed.

'Oh, Thomson,' she cried tenderly.

'You're here now,' he smiled. 'I can't quite believe it, but you're here. Those jealous moments of pure torture...'

'Jealous!'

'Jealous,' he smiled down at her. 'How dared it come nipping away at me when I was supposed to be thinking only of business, when you—looking absolutely stunning, may I say?—came into the same restaurant with some male and...?'

'You were jealous?'

'I wasn't calling it by that name, but was well and truly out of sorts that when I'd imagined you having a solitary dinner back at our hotel—I should have known better than to expect you to do the expected, of course—

you come into that restaurant laughing away with some man who was obviously smitten.'

'I've known Charlie most of my life—he's just a chum.'

'I know,' Thomson smiled. But went on, 'The next I knew, you were on the way to charming the heart out of me at breakfast the next morning.'

Was this delightful, or was this delightful? 'Don't stop there,' she begged, and was beautifully, and quite breathlessly, kissed for her trouble; then, looking fairly delighted himself, Thomson was pulling back.

'I wasn't having that, of course.'

'My charm?'

'Your charm,' he agreed. 'I was, naturally, determined not to be charmed by you.'

'Naturally,' she laughed.

'When I caught myself looking at the back of your neck on the way home, and found I actually had a desire to kiss it,' he owned, to her further delight, 'I knew I was going to have to take some drastic action.'

It all fitted in. 'Which is why you asked for any driver but me?' she questioned, remembering how, in particular, he had asked for Frank that time.

'I was in denial,' Thomson confessed. But went on to admit, 'After a week of not seeing you, I caved in.'

'You missed me?'

'It was starting to hurt.' Yancie knew that feeling. 'I should have accepted that Cupid had got me that night I recognised one of the company's Mercedeses outside a party I was looking in at.'

'You thought it might be me driving it?'

'Of anyone, I knew I wouldn't put it past Yancie Dawkins to treat the firm's car as her own.'

'You were angry?'

'How could I be? At the thought that you couldn't be very far away, my heart was starting to speed.'

'Oh, how wonderful!'

'One way and another you've put me through hell, woman,' he growled. 'I even thought I was going mad when I found a picture of you growing in my shrubbery!'

Yancie laughed in utter enchantment.

Then, her eyes going dreamy, she confessed, 'That night—that night you wrapped your jacket round me because of the cold—I knew then that I was in love with you.'

'Oh, Yancie! You knew then, that night? When we kissed, and loved, you knew?'

'Yes,' she sighed. Then recollected. 'You called our lovemaking a non-event.'

'So I can lie too in extreme circumstances.'

'You lied?'

'Yancie, dear Yancie, the memory of that evening, your shyness yet eager loving, is etched for ever in my brain. You'd got me so that when I risked a goodnight kiss before I let you go I knew my self-control was hanging by a mere thread. The next morning, sanity returned, and I decided I had to keep some distance between us.'

This was all so wonderful, so unbelievable and yet, because of the integrity she had witnessed in him, Yancie joyously knew that she could believe him. 'It must have thrown you when I turned up as the substitute driver to take you to Manchester,' she said impishly.

'I confess it was wonderful to see you again,' he replied, 'but that night I so wanted to kiss you again, to feel you in my arms again, that the only way I could handle it was to keep myself aloof.'

'You were aloof in the bathroom the next morning

too,' Yancie teased, trusting more and more in his love the more they spoke.

'Wretched woman. You stretch my self-control to the limits.'

'You said 'This won't do',' she remembered without any effort at all.

'Nor would it. While desperately wanting you, Yancie, I didn't dare make love to you. You'd been unsure before—how did I know you wouldn't regret it afterwards?'

'At the risk of sounding a hussy, I wouldn't have,' she murmured—and was soundly kissed for her trouble.

'You do love me!' he murmured, almost in wonder, when at last they drew a little way apart from each other.

'Is that so incredible?' she asked softly.

'In a word, yes,' he replied. 'When we returned from Manchester, I tried to apply what logic I could find to this emotion that had erupted in me. I was in love with you, heart and soul. But the more I thought about it, the more I became certain that you would never love me. I decided to cut you out of my life.'

'How *could* you?'

'Probably, I never could. But, to my muddled thinking then, you could help there.'

'How?'

'I went over what I knew of you. There was a tremendous chemistry between us which had ignited a couple of times. But you are a proud woman. To my mind then, if you had the idea that I was seeing some other woman, you, in that pride, would mentally tell me to get lost. You would, in fact, help me to cut you out of my life, by...'

'By deciding to cut *you* out of *my* life,' Yancie finished, amazed now how easily she could hop onto his wavelength. 'That was a pig of a thing to do!'

'Oh, sweet love, were you jealous?'

'Not at all,' she so obviously lied so that it couldn't be called a lie at all. 'I just went and played cards with some other men I knew.'

'And I would much rather have been in that kitchen with you than in that recital.'

'You knew I was in the kitchen?'

'I was just coming out to check on you when I saw one of the maids and, reason telling me—depending on your degree of mutiny—that you might not yet have returned from where you'd taken off to, I asked her if anyone was looking after my driver.'

'She told you we were all having supper in a lovely warm kitchen?'

'She did, and at the end of the evening we dropped off Julia, and then I remember nothing else until I regained consciousness—and I was panicking about you.'

'And then there I was,' she smiled.

'And I was so full of joy to see you, I forgot totally all that guff about cutting you out of my life—and asked you to marry me.'

Yancie's smile became a beam. 'That's what happens when you're caught with your defences down.'

Thomson smiled a loving smile at her. 'The only problem with will-power versus a syringe full of something sleep-inducing. I managed to get the question out—but couldn't stay awake to hear the answer.'

Was he again asking her to marry him? Yancie felt that he was, and she now knew that, as she loved him, so Thomson loved her. But this totally alien shyness that seemed to go hand in hand with this love business was getting in the way again—and she was both shy and unsure.

But Thomson was looking at her, a touch of strain there in his look when, as she hadn't answered, he continued, 'I thought, when you didn't come to see me again, that I had your answer, your refusal. But, given that you have come to see me now—in spite of my mother's interference—may I take it you don't believe I was engaged to someone else?'

Yancie took a deep and steadying breath. And repeated back a phrase he had used earlier. 'While I'm willing to concede there's a vast amount I don't know about you, I think I've learned enough to know that...' she broke off—to fly solo '...to know that your integrity is without question. And, while I'll agree that it took me a long while to get there, to get to see it—this love thing is a devil for clouding the issue—I just couldn't see that you would allow yourself to get in the situations we did, a couple of times, if you were serious about someone else.'

'Oh, sweetheart,' Thomson breathed. 'Is it any wonder that I love you to distraction?' Yancie smiled a dreamy kind of smile—it all seemed so totally incredible. Thomson gave her a tiny shake. ' So—*please*—will you marry me?' he asked.

She let go a sigh of a breath. 'Oh, Thomson,' she whispered, her heart in her eyes. 'I'm certain that if you can put up with my mother, then I can put up with yours.'

'I'm going to take that as a yes,' he stated positively.

Her heart was so full, she had trouble speaking. But she managed, 'I'd be glad if you would.'

And Thomson, hearing her choky words, laughed a tender, joyous laugh and gathered her to him, his mouth against her mouth. 'Life,' he murmured positively, 'will never be dull again.'

A month later Ralph Proctor escorted his stepdaughter down the aisle. Behind them, dressed in scarlet silk and lace, and looking beautiful, were Yancie's cousins, black-haired Fennia and red-headed Astra. They had attended to her every need that morning. But now, as Yancie went down the aisle to the man she would marry, Yancie could think of nothing but him.

Tall, dark and straight in his morning suit, he turned as she reached his side, and her heart almost stopped, he looked so handsome. His breath seemed to catch too when he saw her in her exquisite bridal gown. She wore a veil, but he was able to see into her face.

He caught her hand, and, as if he had forgotten the existence of anyone but her, he brought her hand to his lips and kissed the back of it. 'This has been the longest month of my life,' he breathed so only she should hear.

'For me too,' she whispered. And they smiled tenderly at each other, then Astra and Fennia together took charge of her bouquet, and the vicar stepped forward and, amongst joy, tenderness and love, Yancie Dawkins was married to Thomson Wakefield.

They posed for photographs afterwards. 'Thank you for marrying me, Yancie Wakefield,' Thomson murmured lovingly, his arm firm about her waist.

'The pleasure was all mine, Mr Wakefield, sir,' she answered softly.

They both burst out laughing. Never had either of them been so wonderfully in tune—or so wonderfully happy.

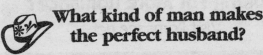

 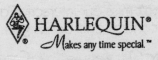

Come escape with Harlequin's new

Series Sampler

**Four great full-length Harlequin novels
bound together in one fabulous volume
and at an unbelievable price.**

Be transported back
in time with a
Harlequin Historical®
novel, get caught up
in a mystery with Intrigue®,
be tempted by a hot, sizzling romance
with Harlequin Temptation®,
or just enjoy a down-home
all-American read with
American Romance®.

You won't be able to put this collection down!

On sale February 2000 at your favorite retail outlet.

HARLEQUIN®
Makes any time special ™

Visit us at www.romance.net   PHESC

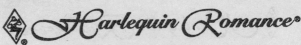

Harlequin Romance®

Coming in September 1999,
the first in this exciting new quartet:

HOPE VALLEY BRIDES

Four weddings, one Colorado family
by
Jeanne Allan

Meet the close-knit Lassiter family—
sisters Cheyenne, Allie, Greeley, and their older
brother, Worth. Wedding bells are set to ring in
Hope Valley, so don't miss:

ONE BRIDE DELIVERED, Harlequin Romance® #3568,
September 1999

ONE MOTHER WANTED, Harlequin Romance® #3576,
November 1999

ONE MAN TO THE ALTAR, Harlequin Romance® #3584,
January 2000

Available wherever Harlequin books are sold.

HARLEQUIN®
Makes any time special.™

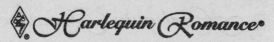